MICHELLE VERNAL LIVES in Christchurch, New Zealand with her husband, two teenage sons and attention seeking tabby cats, Humphrey and Savannah. Before she started writing novels, she had a variety of jobs:

Pharmacy shop assistant, girl who sold dried up chips and sausages at a hot food stand in a British pub, girl who sold nuts (for 2 hours) on a British market stall, receptionist, P.A...Her favourite job though is the one she has now – writing stories she hopes leave her readers with a satisfied smile on their face.

If you'd like to know when Michelle's next book is coming out you can visit her website at *www.michellevernalbooks.com* and subscribe to receive her newsletter.

To say thank you, you'll receive a short New Year's Eve O'Mara family story.

MICHELLE VERNAL

Also by Michelle Vernal
The Cooking School on the Bay
Second-hand Jane
Staying at Eleni's
The Traveller's Daughter
Sweet Home Summer
The Promise
When We Say Goodbye
The Dancer
And...

The Guesthouse on the Green Series
Book 1 - O'Mara's
Book 2 – Moira-Lisa Smile
Book 3 –What goes on Tour
Book 4 – Rosi's Regrets
Book 5 – Christmas at O'Mara's
Book 6 – A Wedding at O'Mara's
Book 7 – Maureen's Song
Book 8 – The O'Maras in LaLa Land
Book 9 – Due in March
Book 10 – A Baby at O'Mara's
Book 11 – The Housewarming coming November 2021

Liverpool Brides Series
The Autumn Posy
The Winter Posy
The Spring Posy – out August 2021

A BABY AT O'MARA'S

The Guesthouse on the Green – Book 10
A Baby at O'Mara's
Michelle Vernal

MICHELLE VERNAL

Copyright © 2021 by Michelle Vernal

Michelle Vernal asserts the moral right to be identified as the author of this work.

This novel, A Baby at O'Mara's is entirely a work of fiction. The names, characters and incidents portrayed in it are the work of the author's imagination. Any resemblance to actual persons, living or dead, events or localities is entirely coincidental.

All Rights Reserved. No part of this work may be reproduced in any fashion without the express, written consent of the copyright holder.

Chapter One

Dublin, March 2001

Tom was like a packhorse bowed under the weight of Moira's overnight bag which he'd draped across his chest. In one hand he was carrying the bag stuffed full of congratulations cards, their daughter's birth bracelet, free nappy samples, a teddy bear and screeds of information on various baby necessities they'd been presented with at the hospital. In his other, he had a death grip on the baby capsule containing his and Moira's precious and as yet unnamed baby girl. He kicked the door closed with the heel of his boot shutting the rest of the world out.

Moira, yawning her head off, was already in the kitchen laying the flowers she'd carted home from the hospital down on the worktop.

Bronagh, who'd just about broken her neck in her haste to peep inside the capsule despite having seen the baby when she'd visited the hospital the day before had asked, 'Moira is that you? Because all I can see behind those bouquets is a pair of legs.'

The flowers were gorgeous but she was too knackered to think about digging out vases for them. Aisling would do it for her. She'd a florist's eye when it came to that sort of thing. Perhaps she could put a few bunches down in the guests' lounge, she thought as her eyes drifted over to the red cast iron pot sitting on the stove. She lifted the heavy lid hopefully and inhaled the hearty aroma of chicken, mushrooms and thyme.

Quinn had made them a casserole!

Her mouth watered. She'd been permanently hungry from the moment she'd given birth and the hospital food had been rubbish though Tom had brought her in a stash of chocolate bars for energy purposes. She felt a surge of love for her thoughtful brother-in-law.

Quinn and Aisling had made themselves scarce when they'd left the hospital saying they'd leave Tom and Moira to settle in with the baby for a few hours.

Mammy had insisted they be there to escort the baby off the premises and before they could make their getaway they'd been ordered to stay right where they were until the photographs had been taken.

Moira had been flanked on all sides as she exited the Rotunda Hospital on Parnell Street. It had been like those scenes of Princess Diana leaving St Mary's in London with the baby William as Mammy ordered them all into various poses for photographs.

The major difference aside from Diana and Charles being royalty was that the royal couple had also looked smart. Diana's hair was done, makeup on and she was dressed prettily. For the era at any rate. From memory, she'd been wearing a green dress with white polka dots and in Moira's book polka dots of any colour were a crime against humanity.

Moira and Tom did not look smart. They looked shell-shocked to be going home seventy-two hours after they'd arrived here at the hospital. It should have been forty-eight hours the nurse had told them given she'd delivered normally.

A BABY AT O'MARA'S

Moira had snorted hearing this because her nether regions felt anything but normal. The breastfeeding was the problem, her milk hadn't come in properly and so she'd stayed an extra night to see if she could be up and running before she went home.

Moira had not been wearing a dress as she left the hospital. She was wearing Mo-pants with a baggy sweatshirt and she'd still got her slippers on. She'd not a lick of makeup on; in fact, she doubted her eyelashes would ever make contact with a mascara wand again and her hair was tied back because it was in need of a wash.

Tom had seventy-two hours' worth of facial hair growth and he'd missed his mouth when he'd snaffled the soup brought in for Moira's lunch earlier. A yellow stain decorated his shirt.

Maureen, however, was done up to the nines for the auspicious occasion of her first granddaughter being brought home.

Donal too had been told there would be photographs and as such he shouldn't wear the jeans with the cowboy belt but rather his good tan trousers. Maureen had debated wearing a hat but in the end, had decided it would be a waste to hide the lovely blow-dry she was after having at the hairdressers.

Aisling was dressed for a day at work and Quinn was in his chef's trousers with the white smock he wore overtop.

'The sooner you all smile, the sooner you can go home,' Maureen bossed clicking away with the camera. She spied a nurse heading for the entrance and commandeered her to take a few shots but after five minutes of Mammy's insisting she'd caught her without her chin tilted just so, she'd had the camera shoved back at her.

'I've patients to see to,' the nurse huffed, striding off.

Maureen had sniffed that the woman's bedside manner needed working on.

When the roll of film was used she'd allowed Tom and Moira to escape to their car but had insisted on supervising to see they'd the hang of threading the seatbelt through the capsule. She was in the know, she bossed because Noah had one just like it and when Tom announced they were good to go she elbowed him out the way to inspect his handiwork. Then they were off with Moira leaning her head back on the seat, eyes closed, muttering, 'Thank feck that's over with.'

She wished she was in the nineteen fifties and she'd be allowed a lovely, long two-week stay in the hospital where the nurses came and took the baby to the nursery so the mammies could all get some sleep. She'd go home full of confidence that she was all set for her new life. Instead, she was exhausted, scared, and her boobs hurt.

The time since her daughter had arrived into the world as a healthy, squalling bundle until now was a blur. It had been a roundabout of Tom's family all trooping in to see her and the baby with an enormous pink balloon saying, 'It's a Girl' and Mammy and Aisling fussing around her. Quinn had popped up as had Andrea, Bronagh, Mrs Flaherty and Mrs Baicu.

In between visiting hours, Tom had given their baby her first bath and Moira had changed her first nappy worrying that her daughter might break given how tiny she was. Then there'd been the breastfeeding debacle. She'd try again when she was home, relaxed in her own environment away from the sound of the other crying babies. She was sure it would be grand then.

A BABY AT O'MARA'S

Moira rubbed her temples as she opened her eyes and urged Tom to slow down. He'd replied that if he drove any slower he'd get pulled over for obstructing the traffic.

It was a very strange thought indeed that the last time she'd been sat next to Tom in his old banger they'd no baby and now there was a real live baby in the back seat letting her presence be known.

They'd made it to O'Mara's with only two irate horns blaring impatiently.

It had been a blessing that Mrs Flaherty had gone home for the day and that they'd only had to get past Bronagh, Moira thought now as Tom set the bags and capsule down on the living room floor. He sat down on the sofa and patted the seat next to him. Moira came over and sat down carefully beside him leaning into his shoulder.

The piercing cry that had abated as they'd parked the car started up once more.

They both sat and stared at the tiny, bundle with the screwed-up pink face.

'What do you think she wants?' Moira asked looking at Tom.

'I haven't a clue,' he said getting up to unbuckle her.

Chapter Two

One month, ten days later...

'Tom, don't be saying 'mix and mingle', that's the sorta thing my mammy would say,' Moira snapped. She was not happy about going this morning, something she was making clear in her tone.

Tom, looking as though he'd be more at home heading off to the beach for a surf than Trinity College's School of Medicine was standing beside the door of the family apartment above O'Mara's Guesthouse. One hand was jangling the car keys in the hope of getting Moira to hurry up and the other was clutching the handle of the baby capsule. His backpack she knew was stuffed full of text books and weighed a tonne.

Sound asleep inside the capsule was their one-month-old daughter whose name they'd finally agreed on was Kiera. Her plump cheeks were pink and her rosebud mouth slack as she slumbered with her chin resting on her chest.

Maureen said she was the spit of Moira as a baby only Moira's head was larger and she hadn't been an obliging baby like the baby Kiera was proving to be.

She was angelic when she slept, Moira thought, a surge of love rushing through her. She resented the fact that instead of curling up on the sofa and trying to snatch an hour's sleep herself she'd been talked into attending a mammy-baby coffee morning. As if she didn't have enough on her plate with her

A BABY AT O'MARA'S

return to college looming and the organising of Kiera's christening; she'd not even had a chance to mull over the guest list. The last thing she needed was to go to a stupid coffee morning where she was bound to wind up feeling more inadequate in the mammy stakes than she already did.

It had backfired on her rather resplendently when she'd told Tom all of this—not the inadequate part obviously because he wouldn't understand that—but the christening, college stuff she'd thought he'd get because he was knackered too. Instead, he'd come back with, yes going back to college would be hard but weren't they lucky with how it had all worked out?

She'd no choice but to agree because they were and the rational part of her brain that wasn't sleep deprived knew this. The part that craved a full night's sleep wondered whether she was doing the right thing by going back to college. How would she cope with full days there, after broken nights of sleep? Was she being selfish going back to college? She was a mammy now after all.

Tom was managing to keep up with his studies and shifts at Quinn's Bistro but she could see the dark circles under his eyes and knew he was running on empty. What would happen if they both burnt out?

Sometimes it felt as though the college thing had been taken out of her hands entirely. There'd not been any round the table discussion as to who would look after Kiera while she worked toward her degree. It had all just been decided.

Moira's mammy would come here to O'Mara's on a Monday. Moira and Tom would juggle Tuesday and then, of a Thursday, Sylvia, Tom's mammy would come to look after her granddaughter and as an added bonus, she was perfectly able with her cell phone which meant Moira could ring and check-in as to how it was all going if she took Kiera out and about. Unlike Mammy.

Even though Maureen had a cell phone—Donal had purchased it for her having gotten sick of hearing her go on about how Rosemary Farrell thought she was the cat's pyjama's because she had one—she'd not bothered to learn how to use it. In fact, the only time it saw the light of day was when she was out with Rosemary. She was apt to pull it out of her bag on those occasions and pretend to use it for the text messaging but really she hadn't a clue.

Moira was not looking forward to the mobile phone training sessions she was going to have to put in place between now and when she started back at college. But, needs must. She couldn't bear the thought of not knowing where her daughter was at any given time.

Aisling was on board for Moira's half day Friday and then the conundrum of what to do about Wednesday had been solved when Nina, O'Mara's night receptionist had offered her services. She'd overheard Aisling and Bronagh discussing the problem and had announced that Wednesday just happened to be her day off and she'd love to look after Kiera.

As for the christening, Tom had said, beaming from ear to ear, it would be great altogether to get his mammy involved in organising it. 'Sure, it's win-win, Moira. She'd love to help.'

Moira had had to butt in and tell him off for sounding mammyish on that occasion too but he'd been undeterred as, warming to his theme he added, 'It will make my mam feel more a part of things because Maureen does tend to take over

A BABY AT O'MARA'S

and Kiera's her first grandchild. It will be a great way for the pair of you to get to know one another better.'

Even though she'd felt irked at being cornered like so, Moira couldn't argue with his point so she'd gone along with it all just as she'd gone along with the arrangements for when she started back at college. She knew she'd be foolish to drop out now but still and all, the little voice in her head niggled at her.

It was hard trying to keep everyone happy and all she could do was hope her mammy never got wind of Sylvia Daly having a hand in the christening arrangements. She'd not wear this news well, especially given she'd volunteered her services. Moira had turned down Mammy's offer of help knowing if she were left to her own devices the christening would take on biblical proportions and had stated that as Kiera's mammy it was something she wanted to organise herself.

She wouldn't think about that now though, she decided.

As for a coffee morning, well, she also knew it wasn't the sorta thing she'd fit into. But it would be nice for Kiera to be around other little babies and as Moira was quickly learning, the world no longer revolved around her.

It was with this in mind she'd dressed her daughter in a particularly sweet pair of stripey pink and green tights, teaming them with a matching T-shirt. Overtop she'd chosen to put on the pink cardigan, that had arrived in the mail along with the myriad cards and other gifts, soon after Mammy had taken out an advert in the national papers to announce she was a second-time nana. Writing all those thank you notes in between Kiera's naps had been very stressful but Moira knew there'd be no peace from Mammy until she'd sent the last of them off.

'Manners are close to Godliness,' was her catchphrase. She'd insisted on using it even after Aisling corrected her and told her it was cleanliness, not the manners.

The cardigan was hand-knitted by Great Aunt Noreen sent from Claredoncally. She and her friends, who, Mammy had informed her were singlehandedly keeping Africa's premmie babies in woollens, had whipped up a variety of hats, booties and cardigans to ensure Kiera O'Mara-Daly didn't feel the cold. From Emer, Great Aunt Noreen's black sheep of the family's niece there'd been a pretty but impractical tutu-skirted dress.

Mammy upon hearing of the gift had pass remarked, 'Common sense doesn't flower in that girl's garden. Sure, Kiera's a baby, not Anna Pavlova.'

The irony of this remark escaped Mammy given she'd Riverdance aspirations for her granddaughter. Moira knew if the black leather ghillies the dancers wore on their feet came in size naught to three months she'd have bought Kiera a pair.

Now she blinked as Tom, affable as always despite his own lack of sleep, grinned and replied, 'You're right it does sound like something Maureen would come out with. Sorry, but it'll be a good craic you'll see. All you first-time mammies together comparing notes. You'll enjoy it,' he coaxed.

Moira shuddered. No, she wouldn't. She knew instinctively she would not be a coffee group sorta girl and he was still sounding suspiciously like Mammy. She used to tell her she'd enjoy the liver and onions but she never had.

She'd been polite on the phone when she'd answered it to hear a woman by the name of Cliona gush about how they'd attended antenatal classes together. She'd gone on to

A BABY AT O'MARA'S

congratulate her on Kiera's arrival before informing her she'd had a little girl too, Fenella, before getting to the crux of her call. A coffee morning get-together for all the new mammies who'd been on their antenatal course. 'Won't it be lovely to get all the little babies together?' she'd chirped.

Moira had found herself agreeing to go even though she fully intended to make her excuses on the day, all the while wracking her brains to put a name to the face at the end of the phone. She'd hung up still clueless as to who the woman was and in a state of disbelief that anyone could sound that chipper with a newborn in the house.

When she'd mentioned the conversation to Aisling, she'd filled in the blanks telling her she remembered Cliona from the infamous evening at antenatal class when Moira's waters had broken on account of Cliona having told Mammy to shush. Mammy hated being told to shush and it took a brave, or stupid—however you wanted to look at it—person to do so. 'She was the big blonde one suffering the Braxton Hicks,' Aisling informed her and Moira had further resolved not to attend the coffee morning.

Tom however had other ideas.

She didn't know why this was such a big deal to him. 'It will be good for you, Moira,' he'd said. 'It's a tough gig being a first-time mammy. You need some outside support.' She'd told him in no uncertain terms that he was to stop practising his Doctor Daly speak on her. Then Mammy had gotten on the bandwagon not to mention Rosi, and even Ash had put her penny's worth in, going so far as to say it would be good for Kiera to be around other babies and she might make some new friends.

How could a one-month-old make friends? And, it was very annoying how everybody seemed to know what was good for her and Kiera. In the end, it had been easier to say she'd go. Now she was regretting her decision.

She zipped up her purple hoodie worn over a white T-shirt. Normally she'd have gone for black but she suspected given her daughter's tendency to spill after she'd been fed, it wouldn't be a good choice.

'Do I look alright?' She'd pulled her hair back into a ponytail and added mascara and gloss which were all improvements on the greasy-haired, no makeup look she'd been sporting of late. She wasn't sure about the cargo pants though. It was strange being out of her Mo-pants. She felt as though she'd been living in those and her pyjama bottoms since she'd gotten home from the hospital.

Night and day had merged into one big ever-turning wheel of sleeping, feeding, bathing and nappy changing. The Mo-pants had gone in the machine with the stretch-n-grows for a much-needed wash that morning. 'Not too casual?'

'It's a mammy-baby coffee morning not a night at the theatre.' Tom shook his head with an amused glint in his eyes. 'You look grand, Moira. You always do.'

She sighed, not knowing why she'd bothered to ask him his opinion because as a man he could never possibly grasp the importance of wearing the right thing. She wanted to look down to earth but at the same time, show the other mammies she still had a sense of her own identity and that she had a handle on this new mammy business.

The fact she was at Kiera's beck and call twenty-four seven, was a walking zombie who had no sense of who she was

A BABY AT O'MARA'S

anymore other than her baby girl's mammy, and hadn't the foggiest idea as to what she was doing when it came to this parenting lark was neither here nor there.

It was all about keeping up appearances. Mammy had taught her well.

She wished Aisling was on hand to ask because her honest opinion could be relied upon but she'd gone to check out a new Glendalough tour and had been spouting the history of the eleventh century round tower she was off to see to Kiera in between nibbling her toast earlier that morning. Moira had told her sister Kiera wasn't interested in medieval towers to which Aisling had retorted that baby's brains were sponges and she'd thank her one day when Kiera was bringing home report cards with an A-plus in history.

Moira had replied that if this were the case then Mammy must have given them all the silent treatment as babies because she didn't remember many A anything's coming home on report cards.

'Come on then,' she sighed now with a glance at Kiera 'Let's go before she wakes up screaming the place down and I change my mind altogether.' She scooped up the baby bag that had replaced her art satchel for the time being and trudged out the door behind Tom.

Chapter Three

Moira descended the stairs to the second-floor landing, noticing how quiet it was despite the guesthouse having nearly full occupancy. The guests would be in the dining room having their breakfasts about now as they fortified themselves for a day's exploring with a plate of Mrs Flaherty's full Irish, she thought.

She was dragging her heels, watching Tom make his way down the creaking stairs and her mind turned to the rollercoaster they'd been on this last while. Her brain had been mush and yet she'd had so many big decisions to make. They both had.

Firstly there'd been the conundrum of what to call their daughter. This had been hotly debated by all family members on both sides before Moira and Tom had announced they'd reached a decision. Their baby's name was to be Kiera.

Mercifully, this had been met favourably although Maureen was adamant it was tradition for the first daughter to be called after her maternal nana. She'd had to concede she'd made this up because not one of her daughters was called Breda after her mammy.

She'd been appeased when Moira and Tom had further announced Kiera's middle names would be Maureen, Sylvia. The order of these two names had been of the utmost importance to her.

A BABY AT O'MARA'S

Then there'd been the time off from college to sort as well as the pressing point of where their little family of three would live. Not to mention the biggest question of all, how she and Tom would navigate being parents. Her head was still spinning as a result.

It had been out of the question that she and Kiera move into the house Tom shared with two other fellow medical students. She couldn't be doing with those eejitty arse flatmates of his policing the shredded wheat and milk. Then there was the fact they couldn't cope with her in the house let alone her baby to boot.

Tom's parents had offered to make room for them which was generous but given they still had his younger brother and sister at home it wouldn't have been ideal. Moira told Tom that while it was a kind offer she didn't think it would be conducive to good familial relations were they to all squish in under one roof.

Mammy, upon hearing this, had put her hand up and said they'd be very welcome at her and Donal's new Howth sea-view, love nest. They hadn't even moved in at the time and were only now beginning to unpack boxes and set up home.

Moira had told Mammy the very fact she referred to the house as hers and Donal's love nest made her answer to that well-meant offer a big fat no. She'd also asked her to kindly stop mentioning the sea view every five minutes. It was very annoying, so. They all knew the house had a sea view and could she not have tacked this news onto the end of the baby announcement she'd placed in the papers and been done with it?

Mammy had replied, 'Child birth hasn't softened you, Moira. You're still a bold girl.'

She was wrong though Moira thought each time she gazed at her daughter and her insides turned to marshmallow. She was changed and she knew she'd never be the same again.

Tom had taken a little convincing that moving in with Mammy and Donal would not be a good thing. He'd liked the idea of a sea view and an experienced mammy to hand.

Moira had told Tom she'd rather stick pins in herself than move in with Mammy and Donal. 'Think of the petrol and then there's the fact she'd be forever telling me what I should be doing where Kiera's concerned. It would be the end of the riding too, Tom,' she'd added. 'I wouldn't be able for it knowing Mammy and her live-in man friend were just down the hall quite possibly doing the same thing.'

The riding had been thin on the ground as it was. Tom didn't want the stables closing up altogether and so when Moira suggested he move into the family apartment over O'Mara's, given there was plenty of room, he'd readily agreed. Moira told Quinn and Aisling it would be good practice for them to have a baby about the place.

As it happened Aisling and Quinn were besotted with their niece and didn't seem to mind her nocturnal waking. Well, not much anyway. Moira flashed back to Aisling's sour expression first thing before she'd had her cup of tea.

Now, as she reached the first-floor landing and spied Idle Ita's bucket full of cleaning products keeping a lonely vigil in the hall, she paused, her fingers tapping the bannister rail.

There was no whining brmm noise from the vacuum cleaner, she thought, her eyes narrowing. She was a lazy mare

A BABY AT O'MARA'S

that one and she'd put money on it Ita was sat on her arse playing that Snake game she was so fond of on her phone.

If it were up to her O'Mara's self-titled Director of Housekeeping would have been long since given her marching orders. It wasn't up to her though and Aisling kept her on at Mammy's behest because she was old friends with Kate Finnegan, Ita's mammy.

Ita, according to Mammy, at any rate, hadn't had an easy time of it when her parents divorced and deserved a break.

You couldn't be a soft touch in business though and Moira knew if Aisling had a penny for each time she'd had to give Ita a talking to over her lacklustre attitude when it came to ensuring O'Mara's gleamed, her sister would be a rich woman.

It was tempting Moira thought to tiptoe down the hall and pop her head around the open door of Room 3 to see what she was up to. Oh yes, she'd like to give her a well-deserved fright. It might galvanise her into doing some actual work.

'Come on, Moira!' Tom called back over her shoulder irritation sounding in his normally easy-going tone.

Moira had to content herself with calling out, 'Morning there, Ita. Hard at it, I hope!'

It did give her a degree of satisfaction to hear the hoover whir into life as she carried on down the stairs.

Her nose twitched at the waft of frying bacon floating up from the kitchen below as she reached the ground floor. The coast was clear she saw, thinking it was like taking part in an obstacle course trying to get out of O'Mara's since Kiera had arrived. Take Mrs Flaherty for instance. She'd wipe her hands on her pinny and hot foot it up the flight of stairs with incredible speed for a rotund little woman in her golden years each time she heard the creak of the stairs just in case Moira and Kiera might have surfaced.

Even if they managed to escape O'Mara's cook there were the guests to contend with. They'd sight Kiera and instantly feel the need to cluck over her and yes, yes, Moira was well aware her child was quite possibly the most beautiful baby ever born but still, it was hard to maintain a cheery equilibrium with strangers when you'd had feck all sleep.

There was no escaping Bronagh though and she braced herself as she ventured forth to where Tom was attempting to move swiftly through reception and out the door to the street beyond.

'Morning, Bronagh,' he grinned, striding past the receptionist. A man on a mission.

Bronagh however was not going to let him make his escape so easily. She was out of her seat with the bowl of Special K she'd been chomping through forgotten about as she nearly tripped over herself in her eagerness to stick her head in the baby capsule.

'Bronagh, if you wake her up there'll be murder,' Moira warned taking advantage of the situation by sidling in behind the reception desk to help herself to a custard cream from the top drawer. She needed sustenance for what lay ahead this morning.

'I've eyes in the back of my head, Moira O'Mara. I'll put a lock on that drawer one of these days or better yet a mousetrap. That would teach you not to help yourself.' Bronagh didn't turn around as she waited for Tom to lift the capsule so as she could stick her head in it and get her morning Kiera fix.

A BABY AT O'MARA'S

Moira watched the goings-on as she demolished the biscuit and wondered if Kiera were to open her eyes whether the sight of Bronagh's face looming at her would leave her scarred. Probably not, she decided. She'd probably think it was her zebra cuddly given the strip of white Bronagh had going on down her centre part.

'Babies love me, Moira,' Bronagh said, her back still to her as she began to make cooing noises. 'I've a way with them.'

'She's not a fecking dove,' Moira muttered.

'No, she's a wee dote is what she is unlike her foul-mouthed mammy.'

Tom grinned, well used to the banter between his girlfriend and Bronagh.

'Don't you dare prod her,' Moira warned brushing the crumbs from her top as she came to stand alongside the receptionist.

'As if I would.' Bronagh was indignant.

'You would and you have.'

'Once, Moira, and I was checking her reflexes.' Bronagh turned her attention back to the sleeping child. 'You're my beautiful little girl, yes you are.'

Bronagh was Kiera's self-appointed godmother. She didn't care that it was tradition for siblings of the parents to be given the role. She'd gone so far as to say, 'Sure you've two sisters and Tom's one, it'll save the squabbling if you just give me the job and besides I'm as good as family, aren't I?' There wasn't much Moira could say to that. It was true enough and she happened to know their receptionist had gone and bought an outfit to wear to Kiera's christening the very same day she'd heard she'd been born.

This news hadn't gone down well with Moira's best friend, Andrea who said she'd first dibs on the role because as she'd put it, 'It's all the go now to have your best friend as godmother and I am your best friend aren't I?'

'What am I going to do about it? She's five godmothers now.' Moira had asked Tom. She'd no choice but to include her sisters and Tom's sister if she didn't want ructions. Tom had said sure, why couldn't Kiera have five godmothers? Andrea had been mollified hearing of her appointment, but had said to Moira on the quiet, 'So, long as yours and his sisters and her on the front desk know I'm chief godmother, Moira, we'll be grand.'

As for godfathers, given Tom had no say in the mothers' part, Moira had left him to it. He'd appointed his cousin Declan from Limerick whom she'd yet to meet and Quinn. When his brothers had heard this he'd hastily bestowed the honour on them too.

Christening convention, it would seem had been thrown to the wind.

Quinn was delighted and taking the responsibility very seriously. Just the other night he'd asked if he'd be expected to oversee Kiera's religious education. Moira had told him that no he would not but a decent present come birthdays was expected.

Bronagh gave Moira a searching glance. 'And where are you off to this morning that has you looking like a smacked arse? It's far too beautiful a day for a face like that, Moira. Don't you know spring is in the air? You should be full of the joy of it, you with a handsome fellow here and a gorgeous wee babby.'

A BABY AT O'MARA'S

Try as she may Moira couldn't inject enthusiasm into her reply. 'A mammy and baby group.'

'Oh, I see.' Bronagh nodded sagely.

'Why'd you say it like that?' Moira asked as Tom edged towards the door, his hand grasping the knob.

'C'mon, Moira, we need to get going.'

She ignored him standing her ground and eyeballing Bronagh.

'I didn't say it like anything at all.' Bronagh fidgeted. 'You've a suspicious mind on you. Sure, you'll have a grand time so you will.'

'That's what I told her, Bronagh. Moira!' Tom pushed the door open, his patience wearing thin as he kept it open by leaning against it.

There was nothing for it, Moira thought, shooting Bronagh one last suspicious glance before trailing out after Tom into the glorious morning sunshine.

Bronagh watched them go and made a tutting noise to herself. Poor Moira, she thought. She might not be a mammy herself but she'd plenty of friends who were and she'd heard them going on about what those cess pit of one-upmanship, mammy, baby groups were like. By all accounts, your first-time mammies were more competitive than a bunch of Irish dancers at a Riverdance audition.

Oh yes, Moira was a lamb to the slaughter –or a lamb amongst wolves or a lamb—she couldn't remember any more lamb adages but all this lamb business had her hungry and she moseyed back to her Special K.

Chapter Four

Tom strapped the capsule in the back of his clapped-out old Ford.

'Make sure you've got it done up properly,' Moira said automatically as she hovered on the pavement.

There was a thud as he straightened and hit his head on the door frame. He'd been about to tell Moira he had it under control but instead swore softly.

Moira decided it would be prudent to slide into the passenger seat and say nothing.

A few minutes later, Tom's mood wasn't improved by the refusal of the Ford to start.

Moira stroked the dashboard and said, 'Come on now, George. You can do it.'

Tom stared at her. 'George?'

She shrugged, 'It's the first name that popped in my head.'

'Could you not have come up with something cool like, like, I don't know,' he shrugged 'but George sounds very old.'

'This car *is* old,' Moira whispered.

'Why are you whispering?' he asked.

'I don't want George to hear.'

They both froze as there was a mewling cry from the back seat.

'Try again, Tom. The engine noise will settle her.' She kissed her fingers and stroked the dashboard once more.

A BABY AT O'MARA'S

'For feck's sake the car's getting more action than me.' Tom turned the key and George purred into life. He stared at Moira in amazement.

Moira gave a satisfied smirk. 'I haven't lost my touch. It always worked when I was a kid and Mammy's car wouldn't start.'

All was silent in the back once more as they inched out into the traffic, which had eased now the morning rush was over.

The trees on the Green were budding once more and on the ground, Moira knew pops of yellow daffodils had begun to appear. She'd never paid much attention to the changing of the seasons other than as to how they affected her wardrobe but yesterday as she'd pushed Kiera's pram through St Stephen's Green she'd seen the world through new eyes. She'd paused to point out the little duck with her downy ducklings waddling behind her in a row before risking the wrath of a park attendant by picking a blossoming flower to show her daughter. Kiera had stared unblinkingly up at her from where she was swaddled in the pram.

Moira settled back in her seat and watched the familiar buildings pass by as they wound their way out of the city centre and stifled a yawn. As they moved out into the suburbs, she continued unconsciously making the braking motion with her foot whenever she thought Tom was being heavy on the accelerator.

It was a habit of Moira's that annoyed Tom no end because he was not a speeder.

Moira, however, was oblivious to the white-knuckled grip her beloved had on the steering wheel and the tense set of his jaw as she continued to brake sporadically and stare out the window lost in thought.

She didn't drive and Tom, along with the rest of her family, all thought she should learn. It would give her independence they said. Everyone had a lot to say where her life was concerned these days, she thought, frowning at her reflection.

She'd had a few half-hearted attempts at getting behind the wheel with various boyfriends over the years but they'd usually ended in tears on the boyfriend's part. This was why, when Tom had suggested teaching her, she'd turned him down flat. They'd had their fair share of drama they didn't need to add driving lessons to the mix.

Getting her licence hadn't seemed worth the aggravation not when she'd always been able to get to wherever she wanted to go in the past. Not driving hadn't been a problem until now.

The thing was, if she were to set about learning now, it would be yet another thing to wrap her sleep-deprived brain around. And yes, alright, she could see that it would be nice to have the freedom and not be reliant on others to take herself and her daughter wherever it was they needed to go. But it, along with everything else right now, seemed like a mountain she hadn't the energy to climb.

Common sense told her if she could drive then Tom could have gone into school early and used the hour he'd spent waiting around to take her and Kiera to this stupid group for studying. It was precious time wasted and time, she'd learned this past month, time was not to be wasted. You had to make every second in between Kiera's needs count and Tom was stretched thin as it was.

A BABY AT O'MARA'S

She recalled Mammy's argument when she'd told her she was grand the way she was and sure didn't Dublin have a perfectly able public transport system.

'But what about when you need to take the baby Kiera to the Irish dancing lessons?'

'Stop calling her the baby Kiera like you'd say the baby Jesus and what Irish dancing lessons?' It was the first Moira had heard of any such lessons.

'The ones she'll be after taking as soon as she's on her feet. You've got to start them young, Moira. You know, like they do in Russia and China. It's a competitive world we live in.'

'But what if she doesn't want to do Irish dancing. She might want to do karate for all you know, Mammy,' had been her rebuttal.

Maureen had shaken her head. 'Moira, Moira, Moira,'

'I might have baby brain, Mammy but I haven't forgotten my name,' she'd said, feeling very annoyed all of a sudden.

'Look at her little legs go when she's under the baby gym. She's a born Irish dancer that one. Not like you and your sisters, you all had two great big left feet and—'

'If you say pumpkin heads, Mammy, I won't be responsible for my actions and sure, Roisin is perfectly able on the dance floor.' Her elder sister was the most coordinated of the three girls.

Mammy was a law unto herself though and Moira had even caught her playing the soundtrack to Riverdance when she'd watched Kiera for an hour last week. They'd had words about covert Irish dancing training.

Now, as a truck's jarring honk sounded she startled and her gaze swung to Tom to see what he was doing wrong.

He tapped the steering wheel.' It's not at me, Moira, yer driver man there's after showing his appreciation for the young one in the shorts prancing along.'

Moira's gaze swung to where Tom was studiously and sensibly avoiding looking at said girl. She might as well have worn a big pair of knickers out and nothing more, Moira thought sniffily. She blamed Kylie Minogue and her hot pants for corrupting Ireland's youth. It was swiftly followed by a Jaysus wept because she was turning into Mammy, now she was a mammy! She'd even be known in the weeks after giving birth to have made use of the four-pack of sensible knickers her mammy had brought up to the hospital for her.

Maybe this morning wouldn't be so bad after all. It might do her good to talk to some other mammies who weren't her own before she began saying things like, 'Did you turn off the immersion,' or, 'you could grow cabbages behind those ears.'

Andrea, despite her pending godmother status, must be getting a little bored with their conversations about the colour of her daughter's poo because, to be fair, Moira would have had no interest in baby poo either until she'd had a babby of her own.

Her phone rang and she hastily retrieved it from where she'd tucked it down the side of the baby bag hoping it wouldn't set Kiera off.

'Hello?'

'Moira, it's me, your mammy.'

'I know who you are.'

'Don't forget to mention the Mo-pants this morning.'

'I will not use the mammy-babby group to market Mo-pants and I'm going to hang up now. I'll ring you when I'm ready to be picked up.' Her mammy had volunteered to pick her up this morning on the condition Moira came home with her to Howth for the afternoon.

'You can look at the sea view while I spend time with my granddaughter,' she'd bossed, 'and Donal will drop you home later.'

It had made Moira think that the driving lessons might not be such a bad idea after all.

She could hear her mammy shouting, 'Mo-pants!' as she disconnected the call.

'This is us,' Tom said, indicating and pulling over.

Moira didn't unbuckle as she stared out at the large Victorian semi-detached house looming to her left. She wondered if Cliona rented or owned. Dublin 6 was a smart postcode. She knew all about property prices thanks to having listened to Aisling drone on when she and Quinn were looking to purchase their rental property.

Would she and Tom live in a smart home like this one day, once he'd qualified and she was painting commissioned canvases?

They were a way off that she thought. How they were going to cope for the next few years was something she didn't want to dive into this morning but she couldn't help but wonder if all the mammies inside this rather grand home had their lives sorted. Was it just her and Tom who were having to take each day as it came?

This was a philosophy they'd decided on during a middle of the night conversation while trying to settle Kiera.

Tom had asked Quinn for his waiting job at the bistro back and Quinn had been only too happy to acquiesce saying Tom was a much-missed asset to the restaurant. Moira had thought it more that Tom's rear asset was much missed. Either way, it was a relief to have his wages coming in once more. She worried about him though because she didn't want his energy reserves to run dry, not when she and Kiera depended on him.

They couldn't live on his part-time earnings alone and he'd extended his student loan; they had minimal living costs at O'Mara's and she'd her student loan too. If things got dire there was always the Bank of Mammy or the Parents' Daly as a last resort, she supposed. They'd both offered to help if it was needed.

Moira had broached the possibility of returning to work instead of college but the idea had been shot down. She'd get her degree, Tom said and Mammy had echoed the sentiment.

When panic about how they'd manage to get through threatened to overwhelm her, Moira would snuggle with her Foxy Loxy cuddly toy. Tom had presented her with it shortly before Kiera was born and it reminded her that the most important thing was they had each other and now they had Kiera too which meant, come what may, they'd muddle through.

'Moira?'

'I'm going,' she barked not giving him his usual kiss goodbye as she opened the car door and clambered out. She managed to free the capsule without too much drama seeing Kiera was sound asleep then she stood there on the pavement clutching it, reluctant to move toward that front door.

Tom leaned over and unwound the passenger window. 'G'wan. Enjoy yourselves.'

A BABY AT O'MARA'S

Moira felt like a child on her first day of school as she walked up the path wishing Tom was holding her hand. He parped the horn as he drove off and she was filled with the urge to run after George but it was too late because the front door was already swinging open.

Chapter Five

'Moira, you made it!' gushed a blonde girl, impeccably made-up in what Moira would call a casual chic ensemble of flowing trousers and pale blue shirt.

On closer inspection, those trousers looked designer she thought as the woman, her hair tucked behind her ears, peered past her. A muslin cloth was draped over her shoulder and a plump baby pretty in pink was resting her cheek against it. The woman jiggled her baby who gave a soft burp. 'Good girl, Fenella. Did Tom drop you off?' she asked, looking past her to the street.

'Erm, hi,' Moira ventured uncertainly. This must be Cliona she thought, vaguely remembering her from the antenatal class. She didn't recall her being this glam though and was surprised by an uncharacteristic stab of envy. She was organised too. Moira always forgot to put the muslin thingy over her shoulder and as a result, had a pile of tops in the wash with milk spills down the back.

Unlike herself, this woman's aura said she had the new mammy business sorted. By comparison, she looked like she was on her way to a girl band audition and had forgotten to drop the baby off on the way. She was regretting the cargo pants and vowed it would be the last time she checked in with Tom for advice on what to wear.

The old Moira would have known exactly what to wear to any occasion and she'd have worn it well. She'd have oozed

A BABY AT O'MARA'S

confidence just like Cliona was. This new Moira wasn't even sure what day it was any more.

Cliona cleared her throat.

Moira remembered the question. 'Oh, Tom, yes sorry he did.'

'What a shame he couldn't have called in for a few minutes. We'd have all loved to say hi.'

Moira smiled weakly. Tom was always a hit with the ladies. Something he was completely oblivious to which was one of the things Moira had initially found attractive about him. That and his bum of course. 'He had a lecture,' she offered up.

'That's right, he's studying to be a doctor, isn't he?'

Moira nodded, wishing her hair was all glossy and shiny. It had been gloriously shampoo advert full and bouncy for the first few days after Kiera's arrival and then it had started to fall out. Now it felt lank and lacklustre.

'He's in his final year at med school.' She didn't add that it would take him another four years to qualify as a general practitioner.

'It must be fab having your own personal doctor on hand.' Cliona's blue eyes took on a dreamy quality that signified she was having impure thoughts about Doctor Tom.

Moira coughed and Cliona blinked, flushing slightly before looking down at the capsule Moira was holding. Her arm was beginning to ache and she wondered whether she was ever going to be invited inside.

'And oh, my goodness this must be Kiera.' Cliona adjusted her hold on baby Fenella and waved her little hand. 'Fenella says hello.'

Kiera obligingly opened her eyes. Moira couldn't bring herself to say, 'And Kiera says hello to Fenella,' so she compromised. 'How're you, Fenella?'

'I'm good thank you,' Cliona parroted

This baby-talking business was going to get old very quickly, Moira thought.

'Your wee one's adorable. I think she takes after her mammy.' Cliona smiled.

'With her daddy's nose.' Moira laughed and it sounded high pitched and not at all like her normal giggle. It was odd standing here on a virtual stranger's doorstep waiting to enter the inner sanctum of the mammy group.

The last time Moira had seen this woman she'd been escorted by her sisters, Andrea, and Mammy from the antenatal class after her waters had broken. In her haste to get to her daughter, Mammy had broken the TENS machine she'd insisted on being connected to, to see if it helped with her back ache. Moira, who'd been in a panic at the thought of her impending labour could hazily recall her mammy being a woman possessed as she ripped the electrodes off. She'd had to buy Yvonne, the antenatal teacher, a new machine which Mammy said was a waste of money given it hadn't done much for her back in the first place and that she'd rather have put the money toward a new wardrobe for Yvonne.

Fair play, Moira had murmured upon hearing Mammy's complaint at the financial injustice of it all. Yvonne had taken eclectic to new levels with her waistcoats of many colours. It had been most distracting and many a class she'd found herself staring at the waistcoat of the week in horror instead of

A BABY AT O'MARA'S

learning how to do something practical like the wrapping of a baby.

'Come on in to casa Whelan.' Cliona finally stood aside to welcome her with a sweep of her hand.

English speaking people who randomly dropped Spanish or French words into their conversation tended to be pretentious gits, Moira thought, noticing Cliona had even managed to paint her nails. She felt chastised as her hostess for the morning added. 'All the other girls are here already. Hopefully, they've left you some of the blueberry muffins I whipped up for morning tea. Breastfeeding makes you soo hungry,' she trilled. 'Us mammies have to keep our sustenance up.'

Moira's heart sank even further. She couldn't imagine baking and caring for her baby. Mind you she'd never baked in her life so there was no reason she should have started now. She'd tried her hardest with the breastfeeding too but it hadn't worked. She hadn't produced anywhere near enough milk to keep her hungry baby fed.

In the hospital, a double breast pump had been wheeled onto her ward and the curtain whipped around as the nurse helped her attach it. She'd cried quietly when the nurse had gone, leaving her attached to the machine feeling like a cow being milked.

Aisling had ducked her head around the curtain and stared at her in disbelief.

'Don't you dare say a word,' Moira managed to sniffle out, mortified. Although she didn't know why she should be. She hadn't a shred of dignity left after having given birth and having had the nurse tug on her boob to see if she could get a decent serving of the Colosseum, or whatever the stuff was called that came in before her milk.

'Oh, Moira,' Aisling had said, sitting down on the bed next to her sister while the awful machine chugged away. Her sister, bless her had popped snowballs in her mouth on demand until the nurse reappeared to see what she'd managed to produce.

It wasn't much and there'd been talk of hiring a lactation consultant after that but Tom had put the kibosh on that seeing how stressed she was.

Kiera was on the formula now and even though she was thriving, Moira felt she'd let her down by not being able to feed her herself.

'Erm, sorry I was late. It's not easy getting out the door these days,' Moira offered up, expecting a nod of understanding as she stepped into the hallway. Instead, as Cliona closed the door behind her she looked surprised.

'Oh, are you not in a routine yet? Cathal and I have been following the *Remember You Rule the Roost* book to the letter. It's a great title don't you think?' She didn't wait for a reply as she added, 'It's been invaluable to us. We had Fenella on a four-hourly sleeping and feeding rota within the first week. By the sound of things, Moira you should definitely take a look at it. Our Fenella's a dream.'

Moira was instantly on the defence channelling her inner mammy, 'Oh, so's Kiera. It was just she was asleep and I didn't want to wake her.'

Cliona wasn't finished. 'Kiera's got to fit into your life, Moira, not the other way round otherwise she'll be calling the shots until she's twenty-one.' Her laugh was an annoying tinkle. 'You can have a look through the book if you like. Paula was flicking through it earlier.' She lowered her voice to a conspiratorial whisper, 'Between you and me she needs a few pointers but I'll ask her to pass it on to you.'

The inference being she needed it more, Moira thought instantly nicknaming, Cliona Clio, the Condescending Cow. Now *that* would make a great title for a book. She managed a quick sweep of the entranceway where she was standing and, if she'd been hoping for a chaotic midden, she was disappointed.

The light and airy hallway wasn't cluttered and the only clue to there even being a baby in the house lay in the pram parked beneath the row of ornate coat hooks inside the door. Moira sniffed and fancied she could smell the faint odour of paint underlying the tummy-rumbling aroma of baking and coffee wafting down the hall. The house was newly renovated, she surmised as Cliona opened the door to the front room and ushered her and Kiera in with an enthusiastic, 'Look who's here, everyone!'

'Hi, Moira,' was chorused by the huddle of women seated on the sofa and armchairs or tending to their baby's kicking on the blankets that had been lain out on the floor. Sunlight pooled in through the enormous bay window and the room, despite being full of mammies and babies felt like it belonged in a show home.

The décor was made up of soft lilac and blue shades just like Cliona, Moira mused, and just like in the hall, there was no sign of the chaos a new baby brought into the lives of first-time parents.

Moira wondered if Cliona had an au pair and she scanned the room for any young European girls. Then, feeling all eyes upon her she mustered up a smile.

'Hi, we made it.' Her eyes bounced from one face to the other, recognising them all from the antenatal group but struggling to recall names. Placing the capsule down, she shook her arm out. The room smelled of babies she thought, breathing in the distinctive, talcum powder scent.

'Tom couldn't make it,' Cliona announced.

There was a collective sigh.

Moira offered up an apologetic smile. 'Lectures.' She shrugged. It was hard work being the partner of a sex symbol she thought, not for the first time.

'I heard you had a baby girl,' a red-headed woman with piercing blue eyes said, looking up from where she was cradling her baby to her breast.

Moira tried to conjure her name. Mary? Mairead? It was something like that.

'Mona,' she supplied reading her mind. 'And this is Tallulah, she weighed ten pounds when she was born. She's always hungry never off the boob.'

As this impressive baby weight was relayed there was a collective wincing and Moira would put money on a mass clenching of the pelvic floor muscles having just occurred. Hers had spontaneously contracted at the thought of a ten-pounder.

Tom had informed her it was important she do the pelvic floor exercises as had her GP when she'd taken Kiera in for her two-week check. They'd both said she needed to incorporate them into her day as often as possible, the intimation being if she didn't then she'd be the sorta woman who had wee-wee accidents every time she sneezed.

The first time she'd sat clenching and unclenching, Aisling had asked her if she was trying not to pass wind and would she

A BABY AT O'MARA'S

not just go out in the hall and be done with it. Fearing she'd be blamed for every offensive odour that circulated Moira had decided to hone her pelvic floor face practising in the mirror. Now, when she did the clenching-release business she looked as though she were silently saying the Serenity Prayer.

'I don't know how you did it, Mona.' A bonny girl with rosy cheeks piped up.

'Gas, gas and more gas.'

This was met with laughter.

'I decided to go natural. I'd heard that was the best for baby,' Cliona dropped in. 'Not that it was easy of course but it was worth it.'

You could have heard a penny drop as all the mammies who weren't able for a pain-free birth stared at their babies wondering if they'd done them a disservice.

Oh, feck off with yer, wonder woman, Moira said silently catching Mona's eye and giving her a supportive smile. Then, remembering to unclench she gestured to the capsule.

'This is Kiera, seven pounds nine ounces. I couldn't very well use the TENS machine after, well, you all know what happened to it and my mammy reimbursed Yvonne for it, by the way, so I opted for the gas too. Jaysus it was marvellous stuff.'

The tension in the room dissipated and there was a smattering of laughter. Several women craned forward for a better look at Kiera.

'And she didn't have a pumpkin head either in case you're wondering,' Moira said reading their minds. 'I think my mammy made that up.' She'd cursed her mammy for telling anyone who cared to listen at the classes that the O'Mara girls carried a pumpkin head gene when it came to babies. She was insistent her three had all been born like so with Moira's being the most pumpkiny of all.

'Definitely not a pumpkin head. She's beautiful,' Mona said, grateful to Moira for having put Cliona in her place.

'Kiera's a lovely name. It means little dark one doesn't it?'

This had come from a brunette with enormous brown eyes to match her hair; Moira had an inkling her name was Lisa. She recalled her suffering fat ankles in her last trimester because Mammy had bent the poor girl's ear about how she was prone to them when she flew and to avoid wearing the tight socks.

'It does, yes.' She was bemused as to how Lisa knew this.

She explained. 'I was going to call Eva here Kiera, I loved it, but it didn't seem right once she was born.' She pointed down to the bright purple fleece blanket she was kneeling next to. A plump baby with a downy covering of golden hair was kicking her bare legs with gusto, full of joy at having no nappy on. 'And she was eight pound four.'

The two women exchanged a smile and Moira liked her, even if she had seemed a tad obsessed with her cankles at the antenatal get-togethers. To be fair, if she'd been the one unable to wear her boots on account of her swollen ankles she'd have been obsessed too.

She snuck a quick glance to see if Lisa's had gone down post-birth but couldn't tell under the cuffs of her jeans. There was a space on the carpet next to her and, picking the capsule up, she edged around the room towards it as more birth weights were compared.

A BABY AT O'MARA'S

'My mammy would have had her called Maureen after herself. She told me it was traditional that the firstborn granddaughter be given her maternal grandmother's name.'

'Really?' Lisa's eyebrows raised. 'I've never heard that before. Just as well my mam hasn't either or Eva would have been called Beulah.'

'Beulah?' Moira bit her lip to stop the laugh escaping.

'My nan read it in a book and liked the sound of it. I always think it sounds like a blowsy, American heiress. Imagine if we'd gone with that, poor Eva would be stuck with Beulah Boyle.'

Moira did laugh this time. 'Mammy made it up. It's not the first time she's invented a tradition to suit herself.'

Moira put the capsule down once more and set about opening her bag to retrieve the paraphernalia she'd need to get her and Kiera through the next couple of hours.

'Tea or coffee, Moira? I've got peppermint, chamomile or I've a lovely herbal tea with fenugreek. It's mammy's little helper when it comes to lactation.' Cliona hovered near the door.

Moira couldn't help herself, 'I thought mammy's little helper was Valium?' Cliona was annoying her so.

Lisa snorted as did Mona.

The rest of the women looked startled and Cliona's eyes widened.

'Erm, I'll have a coffee please, white and one,' Moira added hastily. It had been a joke, sort of. It was going to be a long morning she thought, watching Cliona regroup and put her daughter down under a baby gym an Olympian athlete would have been proud to train under. 'Anyone else like another?'

Orders were placed and a petite blonde girl got to her feet brushing off her trousers, 'Darian's fine there. I'll give you a hand, Cliona.'

'Thanks, Maree.'

The two women trotted off.

Moira busied herself opening her baby bag to pull out the cot sized quilt she'd stuffed in there. She took in the various patchwork patterns and bright fleece material edged with blanket stitches the other handful of babies were lying on. They'd all be courtesy of their first-time nanas or eager aunties she surmised, flapping down Mammy's efforts.

The quilt she'd presented her with looked more like it would be at home on an Amish farm where quilting classes for beginners were being held than in the residential Dublin home she was currently in. It had been made with love and a good dollop of Maureen O'Mara's competitive spirit though.

Mammy had hastily enrolled on a quilt making course at the church hall in Howth upon hearing Tom's mammy had whipped up a beautiful pink, yellow and green blanket for the baby's cot in the weeks before Moira was due. Mrs Daly, whom Moira was now allowed to call Sylvia on account of her being the mother of her first grandchild was a stellar crafts woman. Mammy was not.

Yes, she'd many talents did Mammy but quilting wasn't one of them, Moira thought noticing the large, clumsy joins as she lay Kiera down on it. Kiera looked up at her, gurgling happily, and Moira smiled at her thinking, not for the first time, she had to be the most beautiful baby in all of Ireland.

A smell hit her nostrils then and she realised why Kiera was so happy. With a sigh, she retrieved a fresh nappy and the wipes

A BABY AT O'MARA'S

and set to cleaning her daughter up. She'd surprised her entire family with her non-squeamishness when it came to Kiera's motions.

'I was going to use cloth nappies,' Lisa said watching Moira stick the tags down on the nappy a moment later. 'Better for the environment, cheaper and all that but it went out the window once she arrived. She does the number twos more than five times most days.'

'Five times a day? I don't blame you using disposables. I've no excuse other than I couldn't be doing with all the soaking and washing. I don't know how they did it. My mammy's generation I mean.'

'And don't they love telling you how hard it was and that we don't know we're born.'

Moira grinned. 'All the fecking time.'

'How are you finding the helpful tips?'

'What do you mean?' Moira popped the studs of Kiera's babygrow back together and pulled her tights back up before turning her attention to Lisa.

'The advice. I don't seem to be getting anything right according to my family.' The humour had gone out of her voice now and she looked downcast. 'Ah, ignore me. It's the lack of sleep talking so it is.'

Moira sat back on her haunches and glanced at Eva; she was tracking the brightly coloured, plastic toy Lisa was waving over her, the little bells decorating the side jangling.

'She looks pretty good considering you're getting it all arse about face.' She smiled. 'And I question myself constantly where Kiera's concerned. It doesn't help when I've got my mammy and Tom's mam Sylvia breathing over my shoulder telling me how they used to do things either.'

Lisa laughed. 'Thanks, and I second all of that only in my case it's my sisters. Two of them, both older than me with teenagers.'

'My mammy's got it in her head Kiera will be auditioning for Riverdance by the time she's five and Tom's mam is determined she'll be bilingual. She's forever dropping Italian words in around her. Oh, and now I think about it I get helpful advice all the time. The latest was a little bit of orange and brown sugar would go a long way to helping her when she's constipated.'

Lisa laughed. 'That's a new one on me. The orange juice and brown sugar. Is she Italian then, your mammy-in-law?'

'No, but she went there once on her holidays and loved it. Oh, and she does make a mean lasagne.' To be fair, Sylvia dropped in a delicious pop in the oven and eat homemade tray of the pasta dish once a week. It was a big help. Of course, Mammy, not to be outdone, had taken to dropping in with a shepherd's pie; her specialty or so she said.

Lisa laughed again but then her smile faded and she lowered her voice. 'It's so much harder than I thought it would be. Everybody else seems to take it all in their stride.'

Moira sensed a kindred spirit. 'Not me, I'm not taking it in my stride at all.'

'Or me.' Mona joined in having overheard the conversation. She'd stopped feeding Tallulah and spreading a blanket out she lay her down next to Kiera and Eva.

The trio chatted for a few minutes finding out how each of them had filled their days before their babies were born.

A BABY AT O'MARA'S

Mona was a primary school teacher who confided that she was good with children but had no clue when it came to babies and that it was nothing like she'd thought it would be. 'I thought it would be all lounging about looking ethereal with a baby sleeping on my chest.'

Lisa and Moira laughed and then Lisa chatted about her work for an employment agency. She confided she knew all sorts about managing people but was out of her depth when it came to managing her baby.

When it was Moira's turn she told the girls she'd been a receptionist at a large law firm but had finally found her calling by enrolling in art college to do a fine arts degree. She left out all the messy stuff that had brought her to that life-changing decision. That could wait until she knew them better because she had the feeling she would get to know them better. 'I'd finally got on the right track and then I completely went off course.' She looked down at Kiera who'd discovered her arms and legs. 'Not that I'd change it now of course. It's strange though. I thought I'd instinctively know what to do where she's concerned but I definitely don't.'

Lisa and Mona nodded their agreement. Tom had been right, Moira thought; it was good to chat to other mammies. She could talk freely without feeling she was being judged. It was liberating getting all the swirling emotions she'd had since Kiera's arrival off her chest.

'I'm back to college next week which will be interesting.'

'I've got three months off,' Mona said.

'Me too,' Lisa added. 'Do you feel weird leaving Kiera? My mam had Eva the other day and I couldn't wait for her to take her but the minute she walked out the door with her I wanted her to come back. Although, if I'm honest, there are times I'd gladly hand her over.'

'Me too,' Mona added.

'I think my mammy will have to push me out the door and lock it behind me on Monday.'

Mona and Lisa giggled well able to picture the little woman who'd broken the TENS machine doing this.

'Here we are.' Cliona interrupted the conversation as she bustled in with a tray of drinks and a fresh plate of muffins, her helper Maree bringing up the rear.

'Oh my God. I can't believe she's found time to bake,' Moira muttered.

'I think she's fibbing. They're really from Tesco. I say we go through her bins and look for evidence,' Mona said under her breath and the three women giggled like conspiratorial schoolgirls.

'Thanks a million,' Moira said taking the proffered drink and muffin as Cliona reached her.

'You're welcome.' Cliona placed the tray down on the coffee table and squished in on the sofa. 'Paula, would you mind passing that to Moira, she's having problems settling Kiera into a routine.' She leaned toward a woman ensconced in the armchair opposite. She'd her nose buried in a book.

Moira opened and closed her mouth; she'd never said that.

Paula got up to pass the baby book to her and she took it with a begrudging thank you.

Lisa glanced over Moira's shoulder as she turned to a random chapter and choked. 'Christ on a bike, they're not robots.'

'Crock of shite that,' Mona muttered.

A BABY AT O'MARA'S

Moira scanned the first couple of paragraphs. It read like a baby boot camp. She snapped the book shut and handed it back to Paula with a 'Good luck with that.'.

Kiera had begun grizzling and realising it was time to feed her she made up the bottle. 'Would you mind keeping an eye on her while I heat this up?' She looked from Mona to Lisa who waved her away. 'Excuse me, Cliona,' she said getting to her feet, 'Could I borrow your microwave to heat Kiera's bottle?'

'Of course.' Cliona paused her conversation to raise a disapproving eyebrow. The dark-haired woman she'd been talking to had a coiled plait snaking down across her shoulder. Her baby was in a sling strapped to her chest. She personified an earth mother, Moira thought idly.

'Oh, are you bottle feeding?' The earth mother asked, horror on her face.

'I had problems getting Fenella to latch on, Morganna,' Cliona clucked to her, 'but I persevered and I'm so glad I did.' She rocked Fenella in her arms. 'Breast is best,' she added as though Moira wasn't in the room.

There was a nodding of heads and Moira felt her cheeks redden as though she'd been slapped.

'Personally, I'm a firm believer in doing what works,' Lisa piped up. 'These babies make the rules, not the other way round no matter what that book of yours says.'

Eyes swivelled to gauge Cliona's reaction to this slap down but before she could reply Mona spoke up.

'My mam smoked with me and ate all the things the doctors now say we shouldn't touch and I turned out alright.

Sure, the best thing for a baby is a happy mammy and a loving, safe home.'

Moira flashed her and Lisa a grateful smile and left the room. Despite their support, tears prickled as she made her way to the kitchen at the rear of the house. She knew coming this morning had been a mistake.

A million retorts to the sanctimonious comments she'd been on the receiving end of played in her head. The old Moira would have had a snappy comeback.

How dare that stupid woman with her perfect clothes and perfect house make her feel inferior!

She heated the bottle, wondering how she'd manage to give her the bottle now with all that lot staring at her as though she were slowly poisoning her daughter and all of a sudden she felt exhausted. She wanted to go home and if she couldn't go home then Mammy's would have to do. She dug her phone out of the pocket of her cargo pants and hit speed dial.

Chapter Six

Maureen was spending her morning indulging her latest passion—quilting—all the while trying to ignore the 'hers' side of the his and hers boxes stacked up against the wall of the living room here at Mornington Mews. She really should be unpacking despite the pact she and Donal had made. They'd agreed to sort a box together after dinner each evening so as they could decide what went where because cohabiting was about respecting one another's ideas and compromising.

She frowned over at Donal's Belleek Shepherdess complete with crook. She was very much not in keeping with their Cape Cod theme and as such, she'd been given a place partially hidden by the curtains on the window sill after much compromising on her part.

The jury was still out on putting the framed, autographed poster of Kenny in his white tux on their neutral walls. Maureen was angling for a spot in the toilet by the utility room. Mind you it could be unnerving for the guests who used it to have him grinning down at them while they perched on the throne. She'd have to rethink that, she decided.

She pursed her lips trying to remember what she'd packed her cherished canoe woodcarving from Vietnam alongside. Their new distressed paint finish, display cabinet which Stephen from Home Is Where the Heart Is furniture store had assured them had a distinct Cape Cod flavour was looking lonely. She missed seeing the canoe's majestic form and the memories of the special holiday it invoked. The canoe was what she liked to think of as a conversation piece.

The problem was there was no urgency to the task of unpacking, not now they'd set up home with the basics. They'd had the foresight to label life's daily necessities as they boxed their belongings and so they were now cohabitating in a functional house. It was the bits and pieces that remained to be unboxed though which would help turn their house into a home.

They'd opted for a clean slate when it came to the larger items needed to kit the house out. This was because Donal's furniture held memories of his life before he was widowed and while neither of them had any wish to wipe the slate clean, Maureen drew the line at the chintzy patterned soft furnishings Donal's late wife had favoured back in the eighties. As for her furniture it had been bought when she left O'Mara's to suit minimalist apartment living which had never really suited her.

Aside from a guest bed for the spare room and Maureen's bed which was virtually new nothing else would work in their sea view, love nest overlooking Howth Harbour.

They were embarking on a future neither of them could have envisaged at one point in their lives and their house, just like them, deserved a new beginning they'd agreed. So it was, once Donal's house had sold and Anna and Louise, Donal's girls had taken what they wanted to keep, a garage sale of epic proportions was held.

Maureen had taken the opportunity to offload that which she wouldn't be taking with her too. She'd also appointed herself chief negotiator on the day because Donal would've happily taken the first offer thrown at him. Maureen had told him she'd travelled and was a woman of the world when it came to the haggling and she wouldn't be haggled down to anything but a fair price.

As such, they were nicely cashed up when they'd paid a visit to Home Is Where the Heart Is furniture store. Stephen—fine young man he was with his look of Patrick when he was younger—had done well out of them, she mused taking in her ocean palette colour scheme of sofa, armchairs and cushions—lots of cushions.

She turned her attention back to her quilting and focused. The complicated, decorative hand stitching work draped over her lap required concentration as well as her extra strength reading glasses which had a mysterious habit of hiding themselves whenever she needed them.

Donal, lifting up the cushions of the sofa to see if they'd slipped down the side there earlier that morning had suggested she get a cord and hang them around her neck. She'd gotten sniffy with him at the very idea. Two times grandmother and woman of a pensionable age she may be but she was not a doddery nana just yet, thank you very much.

She'd located the errant glasses on top of her head and told Donal he needed to wear his own recently prescribed glasses more often. He wore them for the driving but refused to put them on when he was home and God forbid he should get caught with them on at a social engagement.

It was exasperating so it was. She knew his refusal to wear them all the time despite his clear need to was because he felt glasses didn't fit with his carefully cultivated, Country crooner image. 'Kenny didn't wear glasses,' he'd said when she'd broached this with him.

'Ah but John Denver did,' she'd countered, feeling certain she'd made a good argument. 'And sure, everybody loved the Country Road song.'

Apparently, Donal had no wish to emulate John.

The house had been quiet for the last hour as her live-in man friend had wisely taken himself out to fix a dripping tap at his daughter Louise's and the only sound was Kenny's familiar, gentle serenade.

She was playing the Best of Kenny Rogers on low to soothe Pooh. He didn't like it when she got her quilting basket out as he didn't get a look in once she'd threaded her needle. He could be very demanding could Pooh but then he'd look at her with those big shiny poodly eyes of his and she'd melt.

He'd only nipped at Donal's ankles twice since they'd moved in and the growling each time her beloved entered the room wasn't as threatening as it had been. He'd stopped cocking a leg over Donal's wellington boots each time he was sent outside into the garden to frolic in the fresh air too

Yes, Maureen assured Donal, they were making progress. Pooh was definitely warming to him. Donal had muttered about them having had more trouble with that poodle than they had their children where their relationship was concerned. She'd had to agree. He was what you'd call a high maintenance pet.

While Pooh's jealousy issues where Donal was concerned were settling down he had developed a worrying twitch since the move. It was twitchy enough for Maureen to have carted him off to their vet.

Mr Feehan had suggested a change of diet could help with the anxiety Pooh was experiencing around having moved house

A BABY AT O'MARA'S

and having another male permanently under the same roof. It was only to be expected he'd said, the pound signs lighting up his eyes.

When she'd seen the price of the doggy biscuits he'd recommended, Maureen had shrieked at him. 'Jaysus, Mary and Joseph, are they suitable for human consumption because the price of them I could be doing with some myself!' She'd fanned herself with her hand for effect but he'd not offered her a discount and had assumed she was referencing Pooh having broken wind. The biscuits would help with that too, he'd assured her.

Maureen made the mistake of confiding all of this to Aisling who'd thought it hysterical and was now telling anyone who cared to listen, that her mammy's poodle was on the medical marijuana. She thought it made a very entertaining story.

Now, she glanced up from her needlework and eyed Pooh. He was giving off happy, poodly snores along with other things. The much-hyped biscuits had yet to help with *that* problem but the twitching, mercifully, had stopped. To be rid of that was worth her personally funding Mr Feehan's pending retirement she'd decided having gone back to the vet to order a kilo sized bag.

She went back to her stitching humming along to *Lady*, when the sudden shrilling of the telephone saw her prick herself with the needle and veer off course with her stitching. Maureen put the quilt down annoyed. She'd have to unpick it later. There couldn't be anything slapdash about it because she wanted to enter it into the Memories section of the Howth Hand Quilters Association annual competition.

It was particularly important she bring home a gold ribbon because Rosemary Farrell, having caught on to Maureen's venture into the world of quilting, had decided to join the association. She'd put her name down as an entrant the minute she'd spotted Maureen's name on the list. She didn't even have a new baby in the family to be quilting for. It was very annoying as was this sudden interruption and, sucking on her finger, she got up.

She answered the phone to Moira's voice demanding to be picked up from the Ranelagh address where the coffee morning she and Tom had talked her into going was being held. There'd been no chit-chat just a 'Mammy come and pick me up now' before she'd disconnected the call.

Maureen put the phone back on its charger feeling even more aggrieved. She'd be having a word with that daughter of hers over her lack of manners. Moira's tone of voice had had the same inflection it would get as a small child when she came tattling tales about her sisters having been mean to her. She wasn't the brightest bulb in the box at times and, Moira had never grasped the fact that given Aisling and Roisin were older, they'd always get the better of her.

Sure, look at the time she'd lisped that Aisling had said the 'F word to her. When Maureen had asked Aisling if this was true she'd wisely denied all knowledge of any such incident. Moira however, indignant, had put her hands on her hips turned to her mammy and said, 'She fecking well did say it, Mammy.'

Maureen shook her head. She still had a mouth on her like a sewer that one. With a sigh, she folded her handiwork. This

A BABY AT O'MARA'S

creation was for Moira although at this moment in time she wasn't feeling inclined to give it to her.

It was extra special because in keeping with the Memories theme of the competition she was cobbling together pieces of Moira's childhood. There was a square of fabric from her the blanky she couldn't be without as a tot and various favourite little dresses she'd worn when she was little. Maureen hadn't been able to part with them.

She put the work-in-progress back in the basket and stowed it away not wanting Moira to clap eyes on it and the surprise to be spoiled. Then, she kicked off her slippers and slid into the boat shoes she was favouring now spring was here. A brief search ensued while she tried to locate the car keys which were like her glasses and had a life of their own.

'We've got elves so we have. Little magic elves that sneak in when my back's turned and move things about,' she muttered into the silence, her hands at last alighting on the keys in the pocket of her jacket.

Moira really was going to have to learn to drive. She'd told Donal this very same thing that morning over their breakfast. She couldn't be dropping everything every time her daughter wanted to venture out and Tom couldn't be hanging around of a morning waiting to take her wherever it was she was wanting to go. He'd enough on his plate with fitting the study in between working at Quinn's, a new baby, and Moira's demands of which she was sure there were plenty.

Jangling the keys in her hand, she headed towards the door. She was having flashbacks to when her children were teenagers. She'd debated having, 'I'm not running a taxi service, you know' tattooed on her forehead and now here she was ferrying her youngest child about once more.

She'd volunteered to pick her up this once because she'd agreed with Tom that it would do Moira good to get out and about and meet some other mammies. The plan was for Moira and Kiera to come home with her for the afternoon and then Donal would run them back to O'Mara's in time for their dinner. She'd whipped up one of her cottage pies for Moira to take home with her and for lunch, she'd hard-boiled eggs to make sandwiches with. Moira was partial to her egg sandwiches.

She was looking forward to spending the afternoon with Kiera and would suggest Moira make the most of having her mammy on hand by having a nap. That way, she could play her *Riverdance: Music from the Show* CD.

Kiera's little legs kicked like the clappers when the Firedance wan came on. Pooh wouldn't like it. He always howled when she played the Riverdance but her granddaughter's future had to take priority. She'd toss his squeaky toy in the garden and he could romp out there for the duration of the CD, she decided, closing the front door behind her and stepping out onto the gravelled path of Mornington Mews.

Mornington Mews rolled around silently in her head. It had such a delightful ring to it. She knew Rosemary was pea green over her having a live-in man friend, a sea view and a house with a name to boot.

Moira had suggested Rosemary could call her home which overlooked the local Spa shop Farrelly Towers. It had taken Maureen a moment but then she'd made the *Fawlty Towers* connection and had giggled to herself. She doubted Rosemary would think it funny, though and, so she'd kept it to herself.

Amanda, she definitely wasn't a Mandy, their neighbour was pruning the conifers she'd placed either side of her and Terence's, he definitely wasn't a Terry, front door.

They were a retired couple who'd been in business and had been the last to move into Mornington Mews. They lived in the middle of the three townhouses in the converted Edwardian manor house.

A young rather yuppyish couple called Owen and Tanya lived at the end. Moira, watching them hare off down the long gravel drive in their convertible the last time she'd visited, had said they needed to wind their necks in the pair of them. She was betting they were something in finance because they'd that sorta air about them. Maureen was inclined to agree. She wondered what Moira would say when she saw them heading off in their beach jeep reserved for weekend pursuits. They hadn't seemed to grasp the fact they were living in Howth, not Malibu.

She and Donal planned on having an intimate soiree for the residents of Mornington Mews once the last of the boxes was unpacked and they'd their new home ship-shape. They were also planning a housewarming but it would be nice to get to know their neighbours a little better before the party.

'How're ye, Amanda?'

'Oh, hello there, Maureen, I'm grand thank you.' She held up her secateurs, 'I've been working out the back and thought it was time the conifers had a re-shape. How's that gorgeous new granddaughter of yours?'

Owen and Katy had a gardener come and shape the circular boxwoods framing their door before he carted his lawnmower around the back. She glanced back over her shoulder at her own front door. Boxwood and conifers were covered perhaps she should look into bonsai. Now, they'd be a talking point. Two little matching bonsai trees. She'd have to ask Donal what his thoughts were on the miniature Japanese trees. She realised Amanda was looking at her expectantly.

'The baby Kiera's a delight thank you, Amanda. Did I tell you I think she's a future Irish dancing?'

'You did, yes.' Amanda shaded her blue eyes from the late morning sun as she gazed up at her neighbour. Tendrils of sandy, red hair peeped out from under her sun hat and her pale, freckled face was bare of makeup. Her trim, no-nonsense frame was dressed for gardening.

The two women whiled away a few minutes discussing the merits of Michael Flaherty jigging about in tight trousers before Maureen remembered she was supposed to be collecting Moira and Kiera.

'I'd best get a move on, Amanda.' She waved to her neighbour and a minute later was crunching over the gravel before nosing the car in the direction of Ranelagh.

Chapter Seven

Moira, telling her mammy what an awful morning she'd had, was fiddling around in the back seat of her car for the seatbelt. The new sticker on Mammy's rear windscreen hadn't escaped her notice.

'Baby on Board.' It sat alongside the 'Best Nana Ever' decal that had been stuck on the day Kiera was born.

Kiera, her eyes beginning to close as she hovered between sleep and wakefulness was quiet as a mouse. Maureen watched in the rear-view mirror as the safety belt was stretched across the baby carrier before Moira threaded it through and clipped it into place. Now wasn't a good time to ask if she'd slipped in a good word about the Mo-pants she decided.

As Moira struggled with the belt, Maureen thought to herself you needed special ops training in order to operate all the paraphernalia babies came with these days. Hadn't it taken her and Donal longer to put up the port-a-cot they'd bought than it had to assemble the new Ikea, Cape Cod-style chairs for the garden and everybody knew what a nightmare furniture assembly was.

'It can't have been that bad,' Maureen said into the rear vision mirror which she'd angled so as she could see Moira. 'It was a coffee morning, there'd have been cakes.' Nothing could be that bad if there were cakes, she thought. She wondered if they were the little fairy ones with white icing or perhaps they'd just had a sprinkle of icing sugar on top. She was partial to a fairy cake.

'It *was* that bad, Mammy.'

Moira had her tongue poking out the side of her mouth in the way she always did when she was concentrating. Her hair tied back like so made her look younger, Maureen thought and seeing the tendrils escaping around Moira's face reminded her of her youngest daughter's school days. She'd always left for school under her mammy's watchful eye looking chaste only to arrive home with puddling school socks, her skirt two inches shorter thanks to her having rolled over the waistband and her hair staging a coup against the tight ponytail her mammy had brushed it back into that morning. There was also usually a terse note in her school bag about her disruptive behaviour from one of the nuns.

Looking at her now, she marvelled, not for the first time, over the fact her baby now had a baby of her own.

'What was so bad about it?' There can't have been cake, she decided. Moira had been anti going along this morning from the get-go but if there'd been no cake then she was standing with her daughter. A coffee morning with no wedge of something iced and delicious was a disgrace so it was. She imagined Joan Fairbrother from bowls reaction if she were to attend such a function and not be presented with cake. She'd be crying out for a public lynching of the powers that be on the Howth Pier so she would.

Moira's voice wobbled in a most un-Moira-like manner which instantly set Maureen's mammy radar on high alert 'They made me feel like a bad mammy because I'm not breastfeeding Kiera. You'd have thought I was after poisoning her with the formula the look on their faces.' She blinked back salty tears and adjusted the blanket over her daughter who'd given in and was now sound asleep. Despite her blurred vision, she saw Mammy grow an inch as she straightened in the driver's seat.

Feck! Mammy only got taller when she was on the warpath.

As Maureen opened the car door, Moira smacked her head on the frame just as Tom had done earlier in her haste to straighten up. She rubbed the sore spot before stepping around the car to block her mammy's path. 'Get back in the car. You can't go storming in there telling them off.' Even as Moira said it, she knew this wasn't the case. Mammy was perfectly capable of doing just that.

'I can and I will. What gives that lot in there the right to make you feel you're not doing a good job with the baby Kiera? I saw you struggling with the feeding at the hospital. You couldn't have tried any harder and when it didn't work you did what was best for you and your babby. And, and besides,' she spluttered still looking alarmingly tall for a tiny woman in boat shoes, 'there wasn't even cake!'

She was fierce and for a fleeting moment, Moira would have loved to have unleashed her on Cliona and her cronies. A rabid wild wolf on an unsuspecting hen coop, but perhaps she was, being too sensitive. It was a sore spot not being able to breastfeed and Cliona and yer dark-haired plait wan and their posse had prodded it. Hard. She didn't know why other mammy's milk managed to flow like the flippin' River Liffey while hers had been a dripping tap that saw her babby howling with frustration and hunger.

Tom and Mammy had told her she needed to move on from those feelings of having failed her daughter. She was a grand little mammy, they said she just needed to start believing it herself. She sighed inwardly. All this softness inside her was a new thing. She'd turned into a Mr Whippy soft serve cone since having Kiera. It was hard getting used to all the feelings whirling through her.

'It wasn't all of them, Mammy. Most of the girls were very nice. It was Cliona the hostess who came over all holier than thou about the breastfeeding and yer hippy, sling-wearing wan.' She thought of Lisa and Mona, she'd liked them. 'And there were muffins.'

'What sorta muffins?' Maureen's eyes narrowed.

'Blueberry.'

'Humph, we're not American.' The wind was going out of her sails, however. 'Listen, Moira, I keep telling you, your first babby is a wondrous thing. It's all new and they don't come with a manual. They're so precious and you're terrified of not getting things right. We're all like that but we muddle through it and before you know it they've grown up. Sure look it, there's Patrick over in Los Angeles doing well for himself despite me feeling I was getting it all wrong ninety per cent of the time.' She wouldn't tell Moira about the dropping him incident. It would serve no purpose.

'Cliona's not scared she's getting it all wrong.'

'Ah well, from my experience the Cliona's of the world are usually the most scared of all. They're just good at hiding it is all.'

Moira pondered that but found it hard to imagine the self-assured woman who'd hosted their get-together being

A BABY AT O'MARA'S

frightened of anything. Something else occurred to her. 'Mammy, what do you mean the first babby's so precious.' She was concerned that Patrick might be the favourite. 'What about the fourth babby?'

'Ah, well now, Moira, by the time number four's on the scene you're so laid back about the whole mammy business you virtually leave them to raise themselves.'

Moira stared hard at her mammy; sometimes it was very hard to know if she was joking or not.

'Come on then, there's no point us standing here on the street. I've hard boiled some eggs for a sandwich for your lunch and I've a proper cake in the Tupperware. A Swiss roll no less. Donal's partial to a slice of Swiss roll with his afternoon cup of tea. There's none of this American muffin business at our house, thank you very much.'

'Is it homemade?' Moira held her breath.

'No, I bought it from the Tesco.'

She breathed out; that was alright then, Moira thought, waiting until her mammy was safely behind the wheel before clambering into the passenger seat.

Maureen decided now was as a good a time as any to start informing Moira of the finer points of driving, starting with the eejit who'd forgotten to indicate they were turning left.

By the time they reached Howth, Moira was beginning to think Dublin was a city full of eejit drivers who forgot to indicate, drove up people's backsides, and either sped or drove far too slowly. The only good driver out and about that afternoon, it would seem, was her mammy.

Chapter Eight

Moira tossed the ocean-hued cushions aside before flopping down on her mammy and Donal's new sofa. Bliss, she thought, stretching long and admiring the view. She was ready to put the upset of the morning behind her and was looking forward to an afternoon of not having to lift a finger while Mammy tended to her and Kiera's needs.

Light flooded through the French doors into the open-plan living area and beyond them lay a manicured rectangle of absurdly neat, green grass upon which Pooh pranced about. She was assailed with an image of Donal in his wellington boots with a pair of scissors in hand trimming the lawn by hand. She wouldn't put it past Mammy to send him out there to do just that.

Cheerful clusters of daffodils, their yellow bonnets bobbing in the gentle breeze, decorated the wall separating their back garden from the neighbours' and all that was missing from the springtime tableau was a fat white bleating lamb. Beyond the garden, Mammy's pride and joy—her sea view—was the kind of blue where you could pretend you were on your holidays on a Greek island. The movement of the white sails down in the harbour was the only clue that the vista wasn't a still life painting.

Her eyes fluttered shut as she imagined herself sitting in a taverna shrouded by brilliant pink bougainvillea, she'd a sangria—no scratch that, that was Spain. She really was getting

A BABY AT O'MARA'S

as bad as Mammy muddling things all the time. All illusions as to relaxing beside the Mediterranean flew out the window as Mammy's voice trampled into her daydream.

'Moira O'Mara get those great big hooves of yours off that sofa and don't be tossing my cushions about like so. I arranged them all in the storm formation so I did,' Maureen stated as she sidled over to where Kiera, still in her capsule, had been positioned in a sunny spot on the living room floor.

Moira reluctantly removed her feet not sure what the big deal was given she'd had to take her shoes off at the front door. Mammy had gotten very pedantic since she'd moved into her new house. 'They're cushions, Mammy, not works of art.'

'They tell a story so they do. Look,' Maureen pointed to the higgledy-piggledy pile on the floor. 'That one there's storm brewing, that's angry sea and that's the calm after the storm.'

'Fecking unbelievable,' Moira muttered.

'I heard that.'

Moira eyed her mammy through narrowed eyes as she realised what she was up to. 'Step away from the baby, Mammy. Don't even think about waking her up, I'm watching you.' She pointed to her eyes with her index and middle fingers and then at her mammy in what she hoped was a menacing manner.

'As if I would.' Maureen took a step back.

Moira shook her head, she and Bronagh were tarred with the same feather with their penchant for waking sleeping babies that was for sure.

Maureen cast one more hopeful glance at Kiera but aside from her little mouth working as though she were dreaming about her bottle, there was no sign of her being about to wake up. She might as well slap their lunch together she decided, taking herself off to the entertainer's kitchen.

Maureen thought in terms of the real estate brochure when she entered the various rooms of their new home. There was the entertainer's kitchen with marble worktop, the en suite with elegant fixtures, the expansive family space living area and their bedroom wasn't just a bedroom. Oh no, it was an adults' retreat.

She set about peeling and mashing the eggs and five minutes later two plump egg sandwiches and a pot of tea were placed on the table. Maureen called Moira over.

She'd been on the verge of nodding off and would have happily eaten her sandwich curled up in the corner of the sofa, cosy in the patch of sun that had settled on it. She knew there was no show of this happening though and as her mammy asked her if her ears were painted on, she reluctantly swung her legs down and padded across to the table.

She pulled a chair out and sat down, her mouth-watering. She liked her mammy's egg sandwiches; they were made just how they should be with plenty of mayonnaise, chopped chives and enough filling so that it squished out the sides when you bit into it.

She took a bite. 'Mmm s'good, Mammy.'

'Don't be talking with your mouth full, Moira. I didn't raise a heathen.' Maureen slid a cup of tea towards her having remembered to put the spoonful of sugar in it. She'd only started having sugar in her tea since Kiera was born, saying it gave her energy.

They ate in companionable silence and when they'd finished, Maureen refilled their teacups saying, 'I was thinking

A BABY AT O'MARA'S

about our chat earlier, Moira and your Cliona wan put me in mind of Bridie Hoolihan. I hadn't thought about her in years.'

'Who's Bridie Hoolihan?' Moira sipped the hot, sweet tea wondering if she was going to regret having asked.

'Bridie was a mammy from the playgroup I took Patrick along to at St Finnian's Hall. It's not there anymore they pulled it down and put a hotel in its place. As if Dublin needed another hotel.' She sniffed.

Moira was getting an inkling that this was going to be one of Mammy's long rambling stories where even she forgot what the point of it was by the time she got to the end. 'And what did this Bridie do then?'

'Bridie was Teagan's mam,' Maureen stated. 'Big heffalump of a child she was too but I felt sorry for her insomuch as her mammy was always after trying to get her to run before she could even walk. Very competitive was Bridie Hoolihan. If I said Patrick was eating the pureed pumpkin, Teagan would be on the steak and three veg. That sort, you know.'

Jaysus wept this was getting more muddly by the minute. Moira put her cup down in her saucer. 'Mammy, would you get to the point.'

'The point, Moira, is titty time.'

Moira spat her tea and began to cough.

Maureen was out of her chair in a flash, momentarily torn between mopping up the specks of tea on her new dining table or thumping her daughter on the back. Moira's puce face decided her.

'Don't gulp your tea so, is it any wonder it went down the wrong way?' she chided in between thwacks.

Moira blinked watery eyes. 'I wasn't gulping the tea it was you going on about the titty time when I had a mouthful of the stuff.'

'Oh yes, Bridie Hoolihan.'

'Here we go again. God above give me strength.' Moira looked heavenward.

'I don't know what you're getting all het up about. I'm only after telling you a story.'

'Please, Mammy, just tell it.'

Maureen fetched a cloth and wiped the liquid off the table before sitting back down.

There was a cry from the capsule but Moira held her hand up. 'Leave her Mammy, she's only just after waking up. Finish your story.'

Maureen itched to pick her granddaughter up but she decided she'd best keep Moira happy and besides Kiera had gone quiet once more. 'Well now, like I said I took Patrick along to a playgroup which was run by a handful of mammies who believed in play-led learning. A load of rubbish it was but there was nowhere else to take him back then and he was a boy who needed to be kept busy. My friend Aileen and I called them the Mammy Spocks, you know after your Doctor Spock wan. We were forever getting told off for talking instead of playing alongside our wee ones. I don't mind telling you though, Moira, there's only so many Play-Doh winkies a Mammy can roll out.'

Maureen glanced around the room and leaned over the table to whisper as though worried Pat might somehow overhear. 'He wouldn't like me telling you this but your brother went through a phase where he couldn't leave it alone. Terrible embarrassing it was. Every time anyone looked at him there he was with his little hands down his shorts. The Mammy Spocks liked to analyse what the children were doing and why. I told them straight. 'Listen,' I said, 'If I was to delve too deeply into why Patrick is always tugging his winky I'd drive myself potty."

'Not much has changed then where Pat's concerned,' Moira couldn't resist slipping in.

'Don't lower the tone, Moira.'

'I still don't see where Bridie Hoolihan comes in or what any of this has to do with Clio, the Condescending Cow.'

'At the end of the playtime, we were supposed to be all hands on deck with the cleaning up which was a nightmare. I think play-led learning was a term for get out every single thing your toddler heart desires and fling it about the place. Bridie Hoolihan always used the titty time to get out of doing her share. 'Sorry, girls,' she'd say hoisting that great big lump of her child onto her bosom, 'it's Teagan's titty time.'

'You should have yanked her off and told her Teagan could wait.'

'I thought about it, Moira, I did but you'd want to have seen the teeth on that Teagan wan. She was like a two-year-old version of Mr Ed the talking horse. I couldn't do it to Bridie.'

Both women winced.

As Kiera began to make the fact she was now properly awake known, Moira let her mammy do the honours and pick her up. She was trying to figure out what it was about Cliona that had made Mammy think of Bridie Hoolihan but aside from them both breastfeeding their babies, she couldn't find any similarities. It may have been a relatively random story on

Mammy's behalf but Moira was surprised to find it had made her feel better.

Mammy worked in mysterious ways.

Chapter Nine

'Mammy it's time for a lesson,' Moira announced fumbling about in the baby bag before brandishing her black Nokia phone like a weapon.

The lunch things were cleaned up, Kiera had finished off what was left in her bottle and was enjoying a bare-bottomed kick on her blanket in the sunshine. Maureen was ensconced in her recliner—she and Donal had bought his and hers armchairs—watching Kiera's little legs pummel the air. She'd been feeling very relaxed and at peace with the world until that moment.

'Don't be waving that at me like so,' she said, her lips puckering in an unbecoming manner. She was a woman who prided herself on not being afraid to throw herself at whatever challenges came her way but this particular challenge was one she'd have been happy to hurl out the window.

'Where's your phone, Mammy?'

Maureen decided to play dumb. 'Over there.' She waved over at the perfectly satisfactory landline attached to the wall.

'Don't be smart, Mammy, you know what I'm talking about. Where's your mobile phone.'

'And what would I be wanting with that yoke?' Maureen glowered at Moira. That daughter of hers had been like a dog with a bone since she'd put her hand up to look after the baby Kiera on Mondays when she went back to college. She'd even gone so far as to say that if she didn't get the hang of using the thing then she wouldn't be allowed to leave O'Mara's with the baby Kiera while she was on duty.

It was down to Donal all this, she thought mutinously. He'd bought her the mobile phone a while ago and after a few attempts at showing her how to use it, they'd both agreed that the learning of modern technology wasn't doing their relationship any favours. It had lived down the bottom of Maureen's handbag ever since. 'In my day we managed perfectly well not knowing where anybody was at any given time.'

'But it's not your day, Mammy, it's my day.'

Mammy and daughter eyeballed one another for a minute or two, peas in a pod and equally stubborn as each other.

In the end, Maureen gave in but only because she was very much looking forward to having sole charge of the baby Kiera. She dug about in her bag until she found it.

'Right,' Moira said. 'Turn it on?'

'How do I do that?'

'Jaysus wept, Mammy, give the thing to me.'

DONAL BREEZED IN THE front door calling out a hearty hello before appearing in the living room where Moira and Maureen had moved from turning the mobile phone on to how to answer it. Moira was in the middle of telling her mammy that she didn't need to shout her greeting as though the person on the other end was calling from New Zealand when Donal appeared toting an enormous cabbage.

He held it up proudly as though he'd just dug this prize-worthy cruciferous vegetable from the garden himself.

A BABY AT O'MARA'S

'Hello there, it's a grand auld day out there today so it is,' he said looking from Maureen to Moira and thinking rather Moira than him when he saw the Nokia phone.

Moira and Maureen were only too pleased for an excuse to take a break from the training session and they both feigned great interest in the cabbage.

A plaintive whine sounded and all eyes turned towards the French doors where Pooh was staring balefully in at them all. He'd had enough of the frolicking it would seem and was keen to hear all about the cabbage too.

'Hello there, yourself,' Maureen said, smiling coquettishly up at her live-in man friend. 'Moira, I'll put the baby Kiera's nappy on if you let Pooh back in? My word that's a big cabbage you've got there, Donal.'

'Isn't it just. Louise's neighbour tossed it over the fence to me.'

'Good job he didn't hit you in the head with it,' Moira muttered, getting up and stretching before sliding the door open.

Pooh scampered in and paused to glare at Donal before planting himself on his mat to watch as Maureen tended to the little wriggly person on the blanket.

Donal either hadn't heard Moira's remark or he was taking a leaf out of his beloved's book and ignoring her as he carried on. 'Noel's an abundance of cabbages coming through this spring and there's only so many cabbages one man can eat even if he is Irish,' he chortled.

'The colcannon will be on the menu tonight then,' Maureen tittered back looking up from her task. She and

Donal exchanged a loaded look, seemingly very pleased with themselves.

Moira sat back down wondering if she'd ever get used to the pair of them flirting like teenagers with each other. How they'd made having colcannon for dinner sound like a double entendre while Mammy put a nappy on her granddaughter was beyond her.

Donal disappeared into the kitchen and Maureen scooped up Kiera having decided the mobile phone lessons were finished for the day. She made them both comfortable in her chair before picking up the baby book which was still on the table next to her recliner from the last time Kiera had been to visit. She held up the bold images for her granddaughter to see.

She'd purchased the flipbook having read that babies find it easier to focus on black and white images but personally, she was looking forward to when they could move onto the storybooks proper. There was only so long she could stare at a pig or a cow or in this instance a butterfly.

'And how's my little princess, today?' Donal asked homing in on her.

'Kiera's grand isn't she, Moira?'

Moira nodded her agreement.

'And does Poppy D get to have a hold?' Donal was already holding his arms out.

There'd been an awkward moment not long after Moira had come home from the hospital when Donal had held his arms out much like he was doing now and said, 'Come on then princess, come to...' He'd looked to Maureen who'd shrugged because as much as it pained her she knew it wasn't her place

A BABY AT O'MARA'S

to answer and so he'd turned uncertainly to Moira and Tom. 'What should she call me?'

Tom had known this was a question Moira needed to answer and she'd felt all eyes in the room on her as she'd mulled it over.

Her daddy wasn't here in person but she liked to think he was watching over them all, especially his two grandchildren. He'd always be their grandad and she'd make sure her daughter knew him just as Rosi did Noah. She'd learned though since Donal had come into her mammy's life, that her happiness with him didn't take away from the love she'd had for her daddy. Nothing could ever change the memories they shared as a family or the love they'd each had for Brian O'Mara but there was room in all their lives for Donal too.

Besides the more people who loved Kiera the better.

Maureen had begun chewing her bottom lip in an effort to stop herself butting in with suggestions and the silence was stretching long but then it had come to Moira and she'd smiled over at Donal. 'I think Poppy D has a nice ring to it don't you?'

'Poppy D,' Donal repeated beaming. 'I like that, so I do.'

Maureen had done that puffy peacock thing of hers she did when she was pleased and Moira had felt Tom, whose arm was around what once had been her waist, give her an approving squeeze. There was a thumbs up from Aisling and Quinn looked around the room pleased to see everybody was happy. Later when Mammy had rung Roisin to fill her in on the latest family news, her eldest sister had agreed, Poppy D was indeed a lovely title.

The only spanner in the works was Noah. His excitement over the new baby was beginning to wane given all the fuss being made over her. Feeling contrary, he'd announced Poppy D was a dumb name and just because the baby Kiera was to call Donal that didn't mean he had to. He wanted to call him Uncle Kenny. Maureen had tried to talk him into running with the Poppy D theme but Noah was adamant. Donal was to be Uncle Kenny.

'I think he's feeling a little left out of things, Mammy,' Roisin had said. 'Children show their feelings through their behaviour,' she'd said knowledgeably because she was just after reading about this in the parenting book she'd got from the library.

'I'll be sure to make an extra big fuss of him when you come for the christening,' Maureen had assured her eldest daughter.

'Come to Poppy D, princess,' Donal had said then and he said the same thing now. His arms were still outstretched as Maureen made no move to place the warm bundle that was her granddaughter in them.

Moira sighed. 'Share, Mammy.'

'Come on, Maureen,' Donal coaxed. 'I'll give her back to you, I promise. I just want a Poppy D, Kiera cuddle.'

Maureen reluctantly closed the baby book and got to her feet so she could place Kiera in Donal's arms. 'Mind the baby Kiera's little head, Donal, you need to support it,' she bossed.

'I had two of my own you know, Maureen, and I've grandchildren,' Donal replied genially.

Once he was holding Kiera to Maureen's satisfaction and he'd finished having a nonsensical chat with her that involved the repeating of 'who's a bonny baby then? You are, yes you are,' he turned to Moira. 'I had a thought when I was out this morning.'

A BABY AT O'MARA'S

'Was that before or after the cabbage hit you in the head?'

'Moira,' Maureen said, 'the cabbage didn't hit him in the head.' She didn't know where that child of hers got her ideas from sometimes.

Donal took it in his stride, tapping the side of his head. 'It's fine, thank you but, Moira, your mammy's after mentioning you're wanting to learn to drive. Perhaps I could teach you?'

Moira felt irritation surge. 'No, I'm not. It's everybody else saying I need to learn to drive. I've too much on my plate as it is with Kiera and going back to college. There's the christening coming up too.' She hastily added, 'It was kind of you to offer, though.'

'Hormones,' Maureen mouthed exaggeratedly at Donal. 'Pay no attention.'

'Driving will give you so much freedom, and you've Kiera to think about too,' Donal continued.

That was true enough Moira knew. She also knew Donal, a teddy bear of a man, would not shout at her if she braked suddenly or forgot to indicate at a roundabout.

'Maureen could watch Kiera for you while I take you out for an hour or so today. We could see how we get on. Couldn't you, Mo? If it works out, then we could make it a weekly thing until you're ready to sit your test.'

'I could.' Maureen nodded enthusiastically.

'I taught my two girls, I'm sure I can have you cruising the streets of auld Dublin town in no time. What do you say?'

Moira was feeling cornered, a feeling she disliked, and as such, she dug her heels in. 'I don't think I'd have the time to learn, Donal and there's no point going out the once. As I said, I've a lot on my plate with college coming up and the christening to sort.'

'I can help you with the christening, Moira. I told you that.' Maureen leapt in.

The word 'feck' sprang to Moira's mind as she realised what direction the conversation was going to go in. It was time for the fecky brown-nosing. 'I know you did, Mammy, and it was a generous offer, so it was, but sure your plates full enough already what with the quilting, the bowls, the rambling, the golf, the painting, and the line dancing.' She took a deep breath and was about to add sailing and the merchandising of the Mo-pants to the list but Maureen jumped in.

'Oh no, Moira, I've stopped playing the golf on account of wanting to spend more time with Donal here, and I'm not doing the painting anymore. I'd gone as far as I could go with it.'

In other words, Moira thought, she'd run out of places to hang the watercolours they all lived in fear of receiving for Christmas.

'The Mo-pant parties are on the back burner too because they're after putting the price of them up on the market where Rosi buys them in bulk. It's hardly worth the bother now and I'm relying on the word of mouth sales. The rambling won't start up for another few weeks either.' Her brow furrowed. 'I don't know whether I'll be re-joining the group this summer. Donal's not keen on it and it's gotten seedy of late. It puts me in mind of Amsterdam so it does only with hills and sheep.'

Moira didn't know how her mammy would know about seedy places like Amsterdam nor could she draw any comparisons whatsoever between the Howth Ramblers Group

A BABY AT O'MARA'S

and the infamous Dutch city. 'What're you on about, Mammy?'

'Bold Brenda was after seducing Niall with that organic trail mix of hers and they were forever ducking off behind bushes while the rest of us were busy admiring the flora and fauna. Rosemary got in a terrible stew about it but that was only because she'd her sights set on Niall herself. She refused to splurge on the organic snacks though.'

Moira willed the image of Bold Brenda cavorting around the countryside in her tighty-whities away. She looked to Donal hoping for backup but he was gazing down at Kiera once more.

Maureen's eyes narrowed. She knew her daughter well enough to know when she was looking shifty and feigning concern as to her mammy's wellbeing was not in Moira's DNA. 'What's going on, Moira?'

'It's just...'

'Just what. Come on. Out with it.'

'Tom's mammy's offered to help me organise the christening and she has it all in hand.' Moira held her breath.

Maureen's chest seemed to expand as she blustered, 'Well now, she doesn't need to trouble herself so. I'm sure she thought I was too busy with all my activities like you did but I've always time for my daughter and granddaughter. I'm on board now so I am. I'll give Sylvia a call shall I? Mammy to Mammy like and, tell her I'm after taking hold of the reins now.' Maureen got up and returned a moment later with a notepad and paper. 'Right, first things first. We need to make an invitation list.'

Moira hadn't known she was clenching her toes until they began to cramp. Mammy wasn't going to make this easy. 'No, Mammy, Tom wants his mam to organise it so as she feels a part of things.'

Maureen's face bloomed red and she began to swallow air rapidly and Moira knew she would have to take action. She got to her feet and swiftly removed her daughter from Donal's arms placing her back in the spluttering arms of her mammy.

'I think now would be a grand time for a driving lesson, Donal.'

Donal took in his beloved's expression and agreed. 'A grand time indeed, Moira.'

Chapter Ten

Nina placed the bag containing the colourful plastic, linking rings she'd just purchased inside her leather backpack. She was excited about looking after Moira's bebé and Ana had loved her rings when she was the same age. They'd be small enough to keep in the backpack she toted everywhere to pull out when she looked after Kiera. Her miércoles toy she'd thought, handing over the money to the assistant, automatically using the Spanish word for Wednesday.

She did the buckles of her bag up and slipped the straps over her shoulders, scanning the shop floor. She really should be on her way to O'Mara's for her evening shift but the childrenswear section of the Mothercare shop pulled her toward it with a magnetic-like force.

She smiled at a woman flicking through a sales rack of winter clothes as she made her way over to where the new in store spring clothing was displayed. She liked to think she blended in with the other mothers shopping for their babies in the store taking up two floors here in the St Stephen's Green shopping centre. Of course, she wasn't like them and she was fooling herself by thinking otherwise. None of them had left their child like she'd left hers.

Ana would love a new dress for church, she thought as her eye was caught by a pretty lemon pinafore. She made for the rack but before she could see if it was available in a 4 a plush, soft rabbit landed near her feet.

A disgruntled toddler was straining at the straps of his pushchair nearby in a bid for freedom and, guessing he was the culprit, she crouched down to retrieve the toy just as he erupted into piercing howls.

'Is this yours?' Nina smiled and the red-faced tot immediately stopped crying as a strange woman handed him back his bunny.

His mother smiled her thanks at Nina and then said something too fast for her to catch in its entirety but the snippets she caught, 'children', 'shopping' and 'nightmare' were enough to get the gist of what she was saying.

What would she think if she knew her story, Nina had wondered as she searched for Ana's size? Would she smile at her quite so readily if she did?

The fear of being judged by others when she already judged herself so harshly was why she didn't tell people the whole story behind her reason for being in Dublin. It was easier because if she were to speak of Ana she would cry. Her motives were good though, she reassured herself constantly.

She'd decided she would say only what she needed to. It was the truth after all just not the whole truth and it was easier that way. She *had* come to Dublin for work just like all the other foreigners who'd poured in from all over Europe and further afield having heard there was good money to be made in the Irish capital. And, she *did* send money home to her parents. It was to help them through the lean winter months when the tourists had left and the restaurant business was slow but it was also being put towards a much-needed extension to the restaurant.

A BABY AT O'MARA'S

An extension would mean more guests and more money in the busy summer months. What was the saying? Something about haymaking in the sunshine Nina fancied.

She held the age 4 dress up for a better look and decided on closer inspection it wouldn't do after all. The yellow would wash Ana out. She put it back ignoring the little voice saying she didn't have time for this, as she continued to mooch until she found what she hadn't even known she was looking for. She snatched the hanger off the rack and stared at the puff-sleeved, cotton dress with a rush of excitement.

Ana loved strawberries and this dress was pale pink decorated with the plump, red berries. She closed her eyes for a second to picture her skipping along the cobbles, pausing to admire herself in the windows she passed by, on her way to Mass and as the image became clearer the piped music and voices around her seemed to evaporate. Standing there in Mothercare, Nina fancied she could the bells tolling in the Catedral Primada Santa María. They were calling her home. Home to her daughter.

'That's class, that is,' a girl who was barely a woman said, making Nina jump. Her strident tones brought her rudely back to the here and now. She watched fascinated as the girl's jaw worked frantically on the gum she had in her mouth, or gob as these Irish were fond of saying. The little one swinging off her hip was tugging at her mother's hair. She didn't look old enough to be a mama but then Nina was in no position to pass judgment.

'It's for my daughter.' Nina smiled shyly.

'She'll look unreal in that, she will.'

Unreal? Nina guessed by her wide grin and the masticated gum on display that she meant something good. She smiled back and hurried over to the counter, pausing only to snatch up a pair of white ankle socks with strawberries on them she spied on her way to join the line waiting to be served.

She'd post the dress tomorrow along with the usual sum she sent home religiously Nina decided, her eyes watering at the overpowering perfume the woman in front of her was doused in.

Ana was growing so fast she'd probably need new shoes too. Her breath snagged at the thought of not being the one to take her to buy them.

Sometimes, if she closed her eyes and emptied her mind, Nina could conjure Ana's smell just as she could hear the bells of the catedral. The scent of talcum powder and lavender bubbles would tease her.

When she'd first left Spain, Nina had brought the baby blanket Ana declared she no longer needed now that she was a big girl of nearly three, with her. On those nights when the noises of the strange city outside her bedroom window reminded her how far from home she was and the bells wouldn't ring for her, she'd bring it out. She could imagine she was holding Ana's warm little body close as she breathed in the fading baby scent.

She'd gone home only once during her time in Ireland thanks to the cheap flights to Madrid she'd seen advertised in the window of a travel agent. It wasn't enough but to go more often would defeat the whole purpose of her being here.

A BABY AT O'MARA'S

'Madam,' the woman called out and Nina blinked. She'd been so lost in thought she'd not realised she'd reached the front of the queue.

'It's very pretty,' the woman behind the counter smiled scanning the tag before folding the dress with a practised hand.

'Mi niña se verá will look hermosa en ese vestido.' Nina was unaware she'd replied in Spanish.

She received an indulgent smile and a few moments later with the Mothercare bag also stashed inside her backpack, she made her way back outside onto the bustling street. She blinked into the sunshine with a happy heart at the thought of Ana's excitement when her parcel arrived.

A glance at her watch cemented what she already knew. She'd just over three minutes to slide in behind the guesthouse's reception desk. Nina set off at a half walk, half run feeling the familiar sensation she'd tried to stave off with her impromptu shopping, the one she imagined to be a little like drowning, begin to wash away her excitement. A new dress would not make up for the fact that she was not there for Ana.

The row of Georgian townhouses opposite St Stephen's Green was in her line of sight now and, with seconds to spare, Nina burst through the door of O'Mara's.

'Ola, Bronagh,' she puffed.

The receptionist was already out of her chair and slinging her bag across her shoulder eager for the off.

A cardboard cake box sat on top of the reception desk at the opposite end to where the flowers, which had dropped a yellow dusting of pollen on the timber, were in full bloom and had scented the foyer with the gardenias vying for attention next to the roses.

'Hello there, Nina. You look like you've just run a marathon!'

'I stopped at the shops which made me late,' Nina offered up, not elaborating as to what she'd been shopping for. She pushed her sleeves up wishing, she'd worn short-sleeves today but knew if she had, she'd have been cold. It was that funny time of year when you either wound up too warm or cold.

Bronagh flicked her dark hair out from under the collar of her new jacket. She liked to buy a jacket at the start of each new season. Her justification was a new jacket breathed life into one's wardrobe without the need to spend up large. The sage colour of this particular splurge had made her feel full of the joys of spring.

It was Wednesday today and on Wednesday's Bronagh had fallen into the habit of calling in on Leonard's sister on the way home. It was her job to bring the cake and Joan's to have the kettle on. Together they'd put the world to rights in between sips of tea and forkfuls of cake.

Joan had been doing marvellously these last few months and her friendship with Gordon, who lived down the road from her, was going from strength to strength. In fact, Bronagh had confided to Lenny just the other evening that she suspected their friendship might have turned to romance. Joan however was giving nothing away. But while Joan wasn't revealing much, the house in which she and Lenny had grown up was showing a little more of itself with each passing week. The therapy Lenny was funding was beginning to make inroads into his sister's hoarding.

Bronagh couldn't wait for Lenny's next visit when he could see for himself just how far his sister had come this last while.

A BABY AT O'MARA'S

Best of all though was her Lenny's pride in the strength his sister had found within herself to change. It made Bronagh enormously proud of *him*.

It was a wonderous thing to be privy to, she'd think each week as she surreptitiously peeked into the front room, which no longer posed a health risk, on her way to the kitchen. Yes, it needed a recarpet, the whole house did, and the wallpaper was tired but it was showing itself to be a room of good bones as her mam would say. Oh, how she itched to roll her sleeves up and give it a makeover like on the television programmes she enjoyed watching. She kept this to herself though. It was Joan's home, not hers, and there was such a thing as overstepping the mark.

Bronagh wasn't the poetic sort, although having said that, she'd once gotten top marks in the English for a rhyme. It had been all about a glorious spring day much like the one outside today. She'd rhymed sun shining with 'silver lining' which Sister whatever her name was, had been most impressed with. If she was the poetic type then she'd liken Joan to a butterfly emerging at long last from her cocoon of clutter which she'd used to keep her safe from the world. She was finally learning to spread her wings.

Sure, look it there was Joan after having a book launch in a few weeks.

Bronagh would never have believed it of the shy woman whose door she'd knocked on, unbeknown to Lenny, all those months ago, in a bid to get to know the sister he'd never introduced her to.

Joan had been participating in life on the periphery by photographing other peoples' unfolding stories on the streets of the city she called home. She'd an artist's eye alright and these pictures had come to Gordon's attention and he in turn had shown them to his nephew who happened to be in the publishing business. One thing had led to another.

Bronagh was excited. Not only would Lenny be over but she'd never been to a book launch before. It wasn't just a book launch either it was a *coffee table* book launch.

Bronagh still wasn't entirely sure what a coffee table book was but she was telling anyone and everyone that she'd been invited to attend a book launch. She liked the way it made her sound like one of those women who appeared in the who's who and who was seen where pages of the newspaper.

'Did I tell you I'm off to a book launch at the end of the month, Nina?' she asked now.

Nina smiled. 'Si, Bronagh.'

'I'll have to get my hair done of course.' Bronagh raised a hand to pat it. 'Would you make a note to remind me to telephone my hairdresser in the morning?'

Nina nodded.

'And how was your day?'

'It was a busy day, gracias.' Aside from her dash to get here on time her lunchtime shift waitressing at Pedro's in the hub that was Temple Bar had seen her run off her feet today. The tips she earned from the tourists who dined at the popular restaurant buffered her wages nicely. Her hand slipped unconsciously into the pocket of the black trousers she favoured for work. The crumpled notes were safely tucked away in there. She'd well and truly earned them today.

She put her tips towards her living costs here in the city. She had a room she shared with a girl from Slovenia in a draughty old house near the city centre where they lived alongside six others. The less of her wages she spent on sundry living expenses the more she could send home and the sooner she could return to Spain and Ana.

Her life here in Dublin was so different to the one she'd known at home in Toledo but the money was good and the work plentiful. It came at a cost though and each time she thought of the heavy price she was paying she'd feel a stab of pain so sharp it would take her breath away.

'Te ves hermosa en verde, Bronagh,' Nina said, noticing Bronagh's new jacket then realising she'd paid the compliment in Spanish translated, 'You look beautiful in green.'

'Gracias.' Bronagh beamed, using one of her two Spanish words. The second being ola. 'There's a pile of reservations for a tour group booking at the end of the month to enter, oh and watch out for Mr McNulty in room eight. He's the sort who'd cross the street to be offended.'

Nina tilted her head heavenward imagining the short man with the thinning hair pacing his room right this moment in search of fresh things to bring to management's attention.

'Don't be taking any nonsense from him.'

'I thought he was in room three?'

'He was but he complained the bed in room three was no good for his back and Aisling upgraded him to room eight with the Californian king to quieten him down.'

Nina knew the type. There'd been the odd diner at the restaurant over the years who feigned something being wrong with their meal to try and get away with a free dinner. She thought they must be shrivelled, mean people inside.

'You pay no heed if he starts giving out. He's the sort who'd complain if he was hung with a new rope.' Bronagh had no time for his sort. Being a carer made you tough like that she often thought. How could you not grow a little hard around the edges when you spent your time around those who really did have cause for complaint but never once grumbled. Just look at her dear old mam and the stoic way she soldiered on.

Nina frowned, trying to make sense of the phrase, but gave up. Whatever it meant she knew it wasn't good. She hoped their awkward guest wouldn't surface during her shift as she placed her bag under the desk.

Bronagh's mouth watered as she picked the cake box up. She'd ducked out to Cherry on Top at lunchtime and had been unable to resist the Red Velvet layer cake. She'd a weakness for dense fudgy cakes and the cream cheese icing she knew from past samplings was to die for. Come to that, she thought, sailing out the door with a cheery wave, she'd a weakness for all cakes and all icings.

Nina sat down on the seat that was still warm transitioning to her evening role of receptionist as she tucked curly wisps of hair behind her ears. She pulled her uniform ponytail tight before picking up a pen and scrawling a note on top of the message pad for Bronagh to telephone her hairdresser. Then, flexing her fingers, she set to work allocating rooms for the Australian tour party arriving in May as she ploughed her way through the sheaf of faxed paperwork.

Occasionally, the front door would open and Nina would stop what she was doing to greet their guests and enquire as to how their day had been. Of the taciturn, Mr McNulty there was no sign.

A BABY AT O'MARA'S

She enjoyed the meet-and-greet side of her work both here at O'Mara's and waitressing at Pedro's. She'd always enjoyed talking to people and had been accused of being a chatterbox all through her schooling. She'd been waitressing tables at her parents' restaurant, Abello's since she'd turned ten and she especially enjoyed talking to the tourists who, seeking something local, would come to sample her mother's traditional dishes. She liked to hear about their lives and the differences with hers in the quaint old quarter of the small city where she'd been born and had lived until she'd come to Dublin.

Her parents had taken the restaurant over, named for the family, from her father's parents before she was born. She'd grown up with the sharp scents of Manchego cheese and garlic and the tastes of smoky paprika and Serrano ham. Her earliest memories were of sitting on the floor of the kitchen banging a spoon in a pot as her mother kneaded, chopped, stirred and seasoned at the worktop and stove.

The business was always going to be passed down to her father and in anticipation of this, her newlywed mother had moved into the family apartment above the restaurant.

Nina often wondered what it had been like for her mama to live with her in-laws because her grandmother was a strong-willed woman just like her mother. She was guessing there'd been fireworks on occasion.

Her grandfather, whom she recalled as having been a mild-mannered gentle man, happy to walk in his wife's shadow, had died when she was six years old. That was when their home life had changed with grandmother deciding it was hard work that killed her husband. She'd packed her bags and gone to live with her daughter and her family in Madrid. Poor Aunt Regina had had no say in the matter but despite the disruption to their lives, she was a good daughter who knew her duty. Besides, it was her turn to look after the old witch, her father had told his sister.

Aunt Regina often brought her back to visit them. Grandmother would while away her afternoon in her old kitchen sitting on a chair telling Mother the breadcrumbs she'd fried for her migas were too soggy or her cocido madrileño needed more salt. Mother would mutter to herself that a pinch more salt on occasion was a small price to pay for peace. She understood it wasn't easy to hand over the reins.

Nina knew her mother had hoped she would be sitting on that same seat one day telling her daughter to add more salt to her dishes but Nina had wanted a different life.

She'd seen her parents' tight expressions in winter when the tables in the restaurant were empty and the room they rented to the backpackers passing through in search of budget accommodation, empty. The bills still had to be paid and as such belts would have to be tightened. The lines around her parents' mouths would deepen, softening only as the weather began to warm up and the tourists trickled back in.

Nina had wanted to be a teacher but her plans had come unstuck before she'd even had a chance to put voice to them. Now she finally had got away she was more homesick than she'd ever imagined possible.

The door burst open, startling her from her reverie.

'Nina, girl, I'm out of loonies you wouldn't have a couple on you, would you? I want to tip our driver,' a voice boomed.

A BABY AT O'MARA'S

'Loonies?' She'd no idea what Mr Tremblay was talking about.

His wife who'd followed in behind him laden down with shopping bags chastised him. 'You're not in Canada now, Carter. He means cash, dear.'

'Oh,' Nina smiled and retrieved the tin they used for petty cash unlocking it to change the large note he proffered. She counted out a handful of change and some smaller notes pressing them into his palm.

'Thank you,' he said before disappearing back outside.

Mrs Tremblay perched down on the sofa to wait for him while Nina retrieved their room key. 'Have you had a good day, Mrs Tremblay?' she enquired.

She listened to her chatter on about their day at Powerscourt Estate exploring the grounds, lunching and shopping until Mr Tremblay rejoined her.

'Sarah, we'll have to get our As into G if you want to call Maddie and have a word with Justin before our dinner reservation,' he said, picking up her bags and waiting for his wife to get to her feet.

'Our daughter,' Mrs Tremblay explained, standing up. 'It's just after one in the afternoon back home and Maddie will have picked up our grandson, Justin from creche. He'll have had his lunch by now and I wanted to catch him before he goes down for his afternoon nap.'

'The poor girl doesn't want your life story, Sarah. She's got work to do.' Mr Tremblay shook his head and moving toward the stairs added, 'She's got this thing about him forgetting who we are while we're away.'

'I'm sure he won't,' Nina replied but even as she said the words she felt sick. She wasn't sure at all because it was something she'd wondered over so many times herself since she'd arrived in Dublin.

Would Ana even remember she was her mama when she finally went home?

Chapter Eleven

Toledo 1996 – five years earlier

IT WAS HOT, SO HOT Nina thought, feeling her uniform stick to her as she hugged her friend Elena goodbye outside her family's shop.

They were only in early June with a whole two weeks until their summer holidays started and if the weather continued to scorch like this it was going to be a long fortnight.

The holidays were something Nina usually looked forward to counting down the days, hours and then minutes until school broke up for the year. Not this year though. She couldn't even begin to imagine what the future held for her anymore. Everything had changed and it was all her own doing.

'Tell them tonight,' Elena urged one last time, releasing her friend. Her hair was as straight as Nina's was curly and scraped back from her face with a headband. She was also as round as Nina was thin although that would change soon enough. The buttons of her white school blouse strained at her chest. Her mother would have to buy her a new uniform before the start of next term, Nina surmised, wondering what would happen to her next term. Would she even be allowed to finish her year out?

'Promise me, Nina. You can't ignore this. It won't go away if you don't say anything. You know that.'

'I know and I promise. I will.' Nina reassured her but still, Elena's chocolatey eyes implored her.

'Tonight?'

'Tonight.' The thought of unburdening herself to her parents made her feel lighter and sick at the same time.

Elena gave her an encouraging smile.

'Your parents aren't ogres, Nina. They love you.'

'That's the problem, Elena. They love me too much.' Nina had always borne the heavy weight of her parents' aspirations for their only child. Their doting suffocated her at times. It was why she'd been enthralled with Brando when he'd come to stay with them. The freedom with which he was living his life had been alluring. She'd wanted to feel what it was like. Elena, an only child too, understood Nina's sentiment.

The strange thing was, despite the pickle she found herself in, there was also the teensiest part of her that was relieved, not that she'd admit that to anyone not even Elena. She'd spent her whole life expecting to let them down and now that she had she didn't have to wait any longer. That didn't make it any easier to find the words she needed to tell them though.

'Which is why they won't be happy at first but—'

'That's the part I'm frightened of, Elena. My father will hit the roof and my mother will take herself off for the first of many private conversations with God. Then they'll wring their hands and wonder where they went wrong and what they did to deserve this shame.'

Elena knew her parents, along with every other Catholic family in Toledo, would follow the exact same script were they

A BABY AT O'MARA'S

to receive the news Nina was going to have to impart to her parents. It might well be the middle of the nineteen nineties in the rest of the world but in their small pocket of Toledo, it could have been the last century for all that attitudes had changed.

'Yes,' she told her friend, 'there will be fireworks but they're practical people too, Nina, and what's happened has happened. Once they're over the shock they'll help you sort out what you do next. You'll see.' Elena hovered a moment longer. 'Do you want to come in for a drink before you go home?'

Nina was tempted. She was thirsty after their upward climb through the hilly streets but knew, were she to step foot over the threshold, Mrs Diaz would block their way to the small kitchen hidden away at the back of the shop. They'd not be allowed to pass until they'd told her all about their day right down to what their English teacher had been wearing. She was considered quite the fashion plate was Ms Gomez. All the girls adored her.

Elena found her mother's need to be privy to her life annoying at times but Nina told her it came from a place of caring. Her mother was the same. The word suffocating sprang to mind once more.

It was this common denominator that had seen the two girls form a tight bond when they'd been prised from their mother's hands on the first day of 'Infantil'.

All the other children had older siblings overseeing them, or so it had seemed to the four-year-olds Nina and Elena who'd had no one and so had found each other. They both understood what it was to be the subject of intense interest from their parents because there was no one else for them to channel their hopes and dreams for the future into, especially in a town where family was everything.

Soon, Nina would derail all the plans her parents had for her. Soon, she would break their hearts.

Elena raised a thick dark eyebrow waiting for her reply.

'No, gracias. I'll see you tomorrow.' Nina fanned her face watching her friend move under the red awning.

She turned, with her hand resting on the door, to mouth, 'Tell them.'

Nina mouthed back, 'I will.' Then her friend disappeared inside the cool interior.

Elena's father specialised in crafting the antique-style swords their small city was famous for and he and his wife sold them out of their shop in the cobbled lane snaking away from the busy Plaza de Zocodover. Business was brisk this time of year and Elena would have a drink and a snack before taking over from her mother behind the counter while she went home to prepare their dinner. Homework would wait until after dinner.

She and Nina had often talked about what they'd like to do with their lives. They were in the last few months of the Bachillerato at Upper Secondary School and after that, they could begin their training in earnest. Elena wanted to be a lawyer which her mother said would suit her need to answer back and Nina wanted to move into teaching which her mother said suited her bossy predisposition.

Oh, the hours they'd whiled away imagining life as students in the capital city away from the watchful eyes of their mothers, neither of whom could imagine their lives without their daughters under their roof.

A BABY AT O'MARA'S

Nina would often joke with her friend that she wished she'd befriended Catalina on that first day of infantils instead because her family owned a shop a little further down from the Diaz's selling handmade chocolate. Chocolates would have been far more advantageous than swords!

'Ah but Catalina is a sneak,' Elena would joke back. 'She would tell your mother all your secrets.'

Unlike Elena who'd faithfully kept hers but it was a secret Nina knew she would have to share this evening after the restaurant had closed, just as she'd promised Elena she would. This was why she dragged her heels toward the plaza. She had to cut through the bustling square in the historic centre of their city in order to reach the restaurant her parents had run since she was a small child.

Abello's was tucked away down an alley on the east side of the square. This time of year it was busy, with her mother Valeria's cocido madrileño having earned a favourable reputation with the travellers who wanted an authentic dining experience.

Her school bag was beginning to pinch her shoulder and her feet felt hot and heavy inside her clumpy school shoes. She longed to take them off but the cobbles would burn her feet. As she reached the square, she made her way past the umbrella-shaded eateries where visitors sipped from tall glasses, occasionally spearing a fat green olive with a toothpick or dunking a torn piece of bread in yellow gold, olive oil.

The sweet almondy smell of marzipan hung on the hot air and a fly buzzed past her ear in no particular hurry. She watched two old men sitting in debate under the shade of a leafy tree talking as much with their hands as with their mouths in between puffing on cigarettes. Traditional music was playing and a small crowd of casually clad tourists watched the dancers clicking their castanets. The square had taken on a festive atmosphere once more now the visitors were arriving in their coachloads to bear witness to it all.

There was a space next to an elderly woman wearing widow's black and a mantilla on her head who was planted on the end of a shaded bench. She gave Nina a toothless smile as she approached. It was a relief to drop her bag down on the dusty ground as she sat down at the opposite end of the bench. The leaves of the tree behind her rustled as though protesting at the heat and the light seeping through their canopy dappled the skirt of her uniform.

She'd sit here just for a minute or two, she decided, regretting her decision a moment later as she became aware of the old woman's coffee bean eyes boring into her. As her veiny hand suddenly alighted on her forearm, Nina jumped, giving a soft, startled cry.

'No te preocupes, te pondrás bien,' the woman lisped.

Nina stared at her. She'd told her not to worry, she'd be alright. The old woman smiled once more before heaving herself up from the bench. Nina watched her shuffle across the square with her head dipped. Her words had unsettled her and her eyes tracked her until she disappeared under the arch beneath the clock tower and out of her line of sight.

She couldn't sit here forever, she decided, staring but not seeing the dancers, the clicking of their castanets growing more frenzied, as the song reached its crescendo. She needed to go home, and picking up her bag she, set off in that direction.

Chapter Twelve

Toledo, 1996 - Five months earlier

The moment Nina set eyes on Brando she knew he was different. He wasn't like the boys from around here most of whom she'd grown up alongside and who'd proven themselves to be childish and annoying even in young adulthood. They'd teased her and pulled her plait when she was young and as they'd all grown older they'd advanced to the pinging of bra straps.

She and Elena had often lamented their lot, saying there were slim pickings on offer in their town and that the young men of Madrid would have to look out when they finally began their lives properly in the big smoke of their capital city.

The afternoon Brando breezed into town found Nina setting the tables in the restaurant for the dinner service. It was a hot, sleepy Saturday and her parents were upstairs enjoying a few hours peace before the frenetic evening rush of a summer's evening at Abello's. Nina had been restless and had come downstairs to do her chores earlier than she normally would. Finishing them sooner would mean she could go and meet Elena for an hour or so before she was needed back at the restaurant.

The tap on the window startled her from the task of folding the napkins and she glanced up to see a swarthy young man with a red bandana knotted around his head peering in at her.

His hands were cupped either side of his face as he squinted in through the glass pane. His breath was leaving a foggy patch and she'd have felt annoyed that she'd have to wipe the marks he was leaving away if he hadn't been so good looking.

She set the white cloth down and moved towards the door upon which the closed sign was clearly displayed. He'd be enquiring about the room she surmised as she opened the door and greeted him with a bright and cheery, 'Ola.'

She appraised him as she waited for him to explain what he wanted. He was carrying a backpack which was not an unusual sight in town this time of year. She often thought the travellers who carried their houses on their back like so were similar to tortoises. Her first impression had been right too, he was very handsome even if he did look as though he'd benefit from a shower. She hoped her face wasn't turning that deep crimson Elena always said she went when she was talking to a member of the opposite sex. It was very frustrating because often as not she didn't even fancy the fellow. She hated to think what she must look like when she did and this young man here was oh so cute. Wait until she told Elena!

'Ola.' He smiled, displaying even teeth, white against his olive skin, as he pointed to the card advertising their room to let propped up in the window. 'Is this available? I'm looking for somewhere to stay for hmm, let me see, maybe three nights?' He held up three fingers.

'Si,' Nina's heart was skipping about as though she'd had one of the strong espressos the cafés under the red awnings in the square brewed up. She wished she didn't have her hair woven in a prissy plait but she couldn't very well undo it and fluff it around her shoulders. 'Come in and I'll show you it.'

A BABY AT O'MARA'S

'I'm Brando,' the young man said, closing the door behind him.

'Nina.' She smiled shyly before turning on her heel. 'The room is out the back here.' Her tread was light across the tiled floor as she ventured through into the kitchen. The prep work her mother had done earlier was in the fridge or simmering in the oven.

'It smells so good,' Brando said, pausing to inhale the rich garlic aroma. 'I miss my mamma's cooking.'

'Si, my mother's albondigas,' Nina smiled, gesturing to the oven as she referred to the small Spanish meatballs her mother had left to bubble slowly in their tomato sauce. 'They're very popular for the tapas.'

'I can see why.'

She moved forward to the door at the far end of the kitchen. The key was dangling from a hook near the frame and fetching it down she unlocked the door, pushing it open wide and standing to one side to allow Brando to pass through and inspect the room.

He paused for a moment looking about the small but practical space and Nina tried to see it through his eyes. It was functional and spotlessly clean. Nina knew this because it was her job to clean it after guests left. It was also cooler than the kitchen.

A double bed made up with crisp white sheets, a colourful blanket neatly folded at the bottom, was pushed up under the window through which a golden light streamed. The window didn't let in enough light for the room to be bright though and a light would be needed if you wanted to read. This was no bad thing in the heat of a Spanish summer.

A fan stood sentry in the corner along with a dressing table upon which a vase filled with dried lavender sprigs was arranged. On the opposite wall to the window was a bench where a kettle along with a basket filled with coffee, tea, and milk pods and two matching white cups and saucers were placed.

The bathroom housed a toilet, basin, mirror and shower where the water pressure, while not marvellous was sufficient to cool off and wash away the dust of the day.

'Very nice,' Brando murmured soaking it in. 'How much is it?' He turned toward Nina expectantly.

Nina told him the going rate giving him the small discount they granted anyone staying longer than two nights.

'I'll take it, for the three nights, gracias.' He looked pleased as, unclipping the straps around his middle, he shrugged the backpack off and placed it on the bed. Nina watched as the muscles in his back flexed beneath his T-shirt when he rolled his shoulders back with the relief of no longer having the pack weighing him down.

She flushed as he turned around because there was something in his expression that made her feel he knew her thoughts. 'We need a twenty per cent deposit for the room and to take some details,' she stated, trying to be businesslike.

'Of course. Do you take traveller's cheques?'

Nina nodded, working out the amount as she made her way back out to the restaurant. She retrieved the logbook they kept under the counter and told him the figure.

A flash of taut, tan skin was revealed as he lifted his shirt and unzipped the bum bag he had around his waist to retrieve a wad of notes. He counted out the correct amount and pressed

A BABY AT O'MARA'S

them into Nina's outstretched hand. She felt as though his fleeting touch had scorched her, and she hid her uncertainty at the physical reaction her body was having to him by fussing about with the till and making a note in the logbook that he'd paid the deposit before sliding it over to him.

'You're from Italy?' she asked reading his neat writing upside down.

'Si, Roma.'

'Rome!' Nina couldn't help the dreamy expression washing over her face at the mention of the great city. She very much wanted to visit there one day and had done ever since she'd seen an old black and white film where the actress had danced in the Trevi Fountain.

'Have you been?'

'No, I've never been anywhere.'

Brando gazed at her quizzically and then passed the book back to her. 'Would you have a cold drink? I walked from the bottom of the hill and it's very hot out there.'

'Si, of course, Coke, beer?'

'A beer, thank you.'

She fetched him an icy bottle of San Miguel.

He twisted the cap off and took a deep swig. 'That's better. Gracias. Will you join me?'

Nina watched as he pulled a chair out at one of the tables and sat down. All was silent and still upstairs and she found herself nodding. She didn't dare have a beer, opting instead for a bottle of Coke.

He had full, shapely lips she thought as he pursed them to light the cigarette dangling between them. He needed to shave too.

'Smoke?'

'No, gracias.' She'd tried with Elena and had coughed until she was sick. It had been enough to put her off.

The striking match was loud in the silence of the restaurant and as he inhaled, a haze of bluish smoke obscured his face. He looked perfectly at ease sitting there—as though he belonged here at Abello's—with one leg, a scuffed sandal partially hidden by the frayed bottoms of his jeans, resting at an angle on top of the other. Nina could see it wouldn't be long before his knee wore a hole in the denim.

'What brings you to Spain?' she asked taking a sip of the sweet soda to hide her embarrassment at such a silly question. He was a tourist. He'd come to explore of course.

He smiled at her. 'I have a Eurolines bus pass and so I go where it takes me. I've been travelling for a month now. I came to Spain from Lyon in France to Barcelona, then Madrid and now here. I like it very much.'

Nina couldn't imagine just going where the bus took you. 'It must be a good feeling. The freedom I mean.' How wonderful to wake up and decide to move on somewhere new if you felt like it, she thought.

'It is and I want to travel for as long and as far as I can.'

'I'd like to travel one day but first I must finish my studies. I'm going to be a teacher.' She didn't want to tell him she was still at school and she found the fib that she had recently turned nineteen tripping off her tongue.

He was twenty-three he offered up, adding, 'I've just finished my studies and I'm taking a year out before I go back to Roma.' He flicked the ash into the round metal tray on the table.

A BABY AT O'MARA'S

'What's Rome like? I'd love to go there one day.'

'You should. Everybody should visit it at least once in their lifetime.'

Nina listened enthralled as he told her about the sights and smells of his home city. He talked with his hands as much as his mouth and he made her feel as though she were there with him dodging the Vespas, admiring the beautiful works of art, and wiping the mozzarella cheese from her chin as he told her the first thing she must do upon visiting his city was eat pizza.

'But big cities they can be lonely too. It must be nice living somewhere smaller and so beautiful.'

Nina felt proud of her tiny pocket of the world. The longer Brando had talked the more at ease she'd felt and so she found herself opening up to him in a way she'd never done with a boy before. She agreed that yes, Toledo was beautiful but it was stifling too to live somewhere where all the local people knew you by name. She told him she longed for the anonymity of a larger place where she could be free to be whoever she wanted.

Brando lit another cigarette and listened with his head tilted to one side in a manner which made her feel like the most interesting of people as she carried on talking.

She spoke of all the hidden things in the old town that the guidebooks didn't tell you about and that he must see while he was here.

'Would you take me to see them?'

Nina pinched her bottom lip between her teeth as she nodded shyly and they arranged that she'd meet him tomorrow after church in the square.

'Nina, who's this?'

She jumped; she'd not heard her mother come down the stairs. For a large woman, she could be stealthy when she wanted to be.

'This is Brando, Mama, he's staying for three nights.'

'Bienvenido, Brando.' She bustled over, all smiles, to take his empty beer bottle but her eyes when they met Nina's were flinty. 'Nina, I need your help in the kitchen, por favor.'

Nina got up from the table, picking up the Coke bottle and shooting Brando an apologetic smile as she did as she was told. The thought of meeting him tomorrow dispelled the annoyance she felt at the tight leash her parents kept her on.

Chapter Thirteen

Moira glanced at Donal fondly as the car bunny-hopped along. He'd driven them to a stretch of country lane in the middle of nowhere before pulling over so they could swap seats. She'd anxiously fiddled around with the seat before adjusting the rear and side mirrors. All delaying tactics which Donal was having none of. He'd told her to turn the key which she'd dutifully done before following his instructions with the gears, brake and accelerator, giving a squeal of delight when the car began to move off.

They'd been at this driving lark for a good ten minutes now and it was all going very well indeed. He'd missed his calling had Donal. He should have been a driving instructor and Moira couldn't help but think that if Mammy were to take out a personal advert in the papers it would read:

Must have the patience of a saint;
Mustn't mind rabid poodle;
And, must do as told.

And, if Donal were to answer it then he'd fit the bill perfectly.

He hadn't shouted at her once so far during their driving lesson, unlike her ex-boyfriends who'd all vocalised their feelings as to her ability behind the wheel within seconds.

For Donal's part, his knuckles were white as he held on to the dashboard issuing instructions to his beloved's youngest child in an even tone of voice that belied his terror. Sure, he told himself, the worst thing that could happen was they'd wind up in a field.

Either side of them, tangled bramble bushes framed the patchwork countryside, and the earthy smell of animals was making itself known through the gap where Donal had wound his window down so as he could gulp in air as and when needed. The only spectators to the driving lesson were the smattering of sheep milling about over yonder, and they were more interested in the fresh spring grass than Moira's prowess behind the wheel.

Or, at least that's what they thought.

Neither Moira nor Donal noticed the garda car tucked away on a turn-off they'd just passed.

The vehicle behind the wheel of which sat Officer Irma Clancy had been parked up for the last hour or so lying in wait for the local lad who'd been using the private farmer's road Moira and Donal had unwittingly turned down as a personal race track.

Officer Clancy had polished off her sandwiches and, there was not a drop left in her thermos. She was fed up with the smell of manure and was also getting thoroughly sick of the easy listening music programme she'd no choice but to listen to because it was that or the baaing of sheep.

It was the only radio station she could get reception for out here in the boondocks and yer DJ man clearly had an obsession with the Corrs sisters along with the majority of male Dublin easy listening music fans. He'd waxed lyrical about how talented the girls were not once mentioning their poor brother before playing the third song by them in under an hour. When he'd asked listeners to call in and tell him what their favourite

A BABY AT O'MARA'S

Corrs song was she'd been sorely tempted to ring up and tell him she'd arrest him for causing mental anguish as she was now going to have 'Breathless' stuck in her head all day. She refrained though because that would be abusing her position and Officer Irma Clancy prided herself on doing everything by the book.

Her eyes widened as the car juddered past. Drinking and driving at this time of the day was a disgrace, she thought, tossing the empty plastic sandwich container aside as her training took hold.

She nosed the white car, with its distinctive fluorescent strip down the side, out of the laneway, and putting the siren on, she drove up behind the offending vehicle, fully expecting it to pull over.

Unfortunately, the sudden noise behind them startled Moira and her foot accidentally pressed down on the accelerator instead of the brake. The car shot forward and Donal, feeling a little like one of the Duke brothers from that seventies show his girls had loved with Roscoe P. Coltrane in hot pursuit, tried to remain calm as he ordered Moira to brake.

The police car sped up as did Moira and it was only when Donal tossed calm out the window and yelled at her to take both feet off the pedals that the car began to slow. Only then, could he use the hand brake to ease the car into a complete halt on the side of the lane.

The garda car pulled in behind them and the siren mercifully was switched off.

Donal exhaled through his teeth wishing he'd a bottle of whiskey to hand while Moira fluffed her hair and licked her lips. She wished she was wearing something a little more provocative than the purple hoodie she'd pulled over her head that morning but she couldn't do much about that now.

'Don't worry, Donal,' she reassured her mammy's man friend. 'I'll have him eating out the palm of my hand. We'll get away with a slap on the hand and no more you'll see.'

Yes, Donal thought, this was getting more and more like a *Dukes of Hazard* episode as Daisy Duke fluffed her hair and waited to use her feminine wiles on that soft touch deputy, Enos.

Things went off script after that though because the tap on the window signalling Moira should wind it down came from a she not a he. A very unsmiley she at that.

The window rolled down and Moira's heart sank as she received a hard stare from a woman of middling years with a no-nonsense haircut. Moira sensed an attitude to match the hair having already surmised she was the sorta woman who'd tuck her vest into her knickers.

'Erm, good afternoon, officer.' Moira smiled up at Officer No-Nonsense, squinting as she tried to read the name on her badge.

'Licence please,' was barked at her.

Donal cut across Moira, explaining the situation. He apologized for the high-speed chase that had ensued, assuring the gardai officer they hadn't been trying to make a getaway and that it had been a panicked reaction to the siren by a new driver.

'Did you know you're a dead ringer for Kenny Rogers?' Officer Clancy said before narrowing her eyes and staring at the dark-haired wan behind the wheel. Come to that, she'd

A BABY AT O'MARA'S

a look of Andrea Corr about her. The fecking Corrs were haunting her today so they were.

Donal scratched his beard and told the officer she wasn't the first person to say that and he did in fact sing in a Kenny Rogers Tribute band called The Gamblers.

In that way of the world being a small place, it transpired that Officer Clancy, as Moira had deduced she was called, was a huge Kenny Rogers fan. The Gamblers had played at her fiftieth birthday bash last year. It had been organised as a surprise by her husband and a grand night indeed had been had by all.

Moira watched as, despite her fond memories of having seen Donal perform, she still wrote them out a ticket for a list of misdemeanours. The Irish police force could not be wooed it would seem. She wondered if Officer Clancy was wearing a bulletproof vest over top of her Marks and Spencer's woolly vest. She'd be around the age where the menopause would be making itself known. If so, that would explain her surliness. The poor woman was overheating. Mammy had been a nightmare when she'd started with the hot flushing and she was a vest wearer too.

'I think it's best I drive us home, Moira.' Donal said once Officer Clancy had returned to her car. He put his hand on the door handle.

'Ah no, Donal, you know the saying about getting right back in the saddle.'

She'd a point, Donal thought, waiting until Officer Clancy had done a U-turn and disappeared back around the bend.

'Alright but I need something to soothe my nerves.'

Moira didn't argue as he fiddled around with the CDs he had stashed in the glove box before choosing one to slot into the machine. She didn't dare breathe a word of complaint either as a twanging banjo echoed around them followed by some mournful sounding fella singing about his heart having been broken.

Something very strange happened to Moira as she set off once more. She felt calm and the urge to keep jabbing the pedals with her feet had passed. The car was gliding down the lane as smoothly as yer man singing. She didn't grind the gears or stall the car once.

'Donal,' she said braking suddenly as the realisation hit her.

Donal shot forward and back in his seat.

'I think the country music helps with my driving. It's very soothing so. You don't happen to have any Shania Twain in there do you?' Moira gestured to the glove box. 'Because I think I might even be able to learn how to do the parallel park if Shania was singing.'

'Moira, I think we might leave the parallel parking for another day.'

Chapter Fourteen

In a café on the main street in Howth just a stone's throw from the pier, Maureen O'Mara was pontificating about the injustice of the baby Kiera's other nana being tasked with the christening arrangements.

Rosemary Farrell who was enjoying holding the baby Kiera made appropriate aggrieved noises every so often as the two women waited for the cappuccinos and scones they'd ordered to arrive.

Rosemary's Nokia phone was on the table in front of her in case she was to receive an urgent call and Maureen's Nokia was in front of her because she wasn't to be outdone.

She'd be making a few urgent calls of her own before the afternoon was done, you could be sure of that, she thought eyeing the phone. Her fingers twitched with the urge to telephone Aisling to share the heartbreaking news that she'd been pushed aside by her own flesh and blood. She'd have liked to have called Roisin over in London, too but, she wasn't sure what the call charges were for across the water, and the same went for Pat in Los Angeles so Aisling would have to do.

Moira had put her number and Aisling's on the speed dial against her better judgment and at her mammy's insistence. She'd enjoyed entering Rosi's however because she'd been very annoying of late with all her helpful advice.

Maureen was fairly sure she'd the hang of how to use the mobile now and didn't know what all the fuss had been about.

Sure, it was a great invention altogether. What a thing to be able to telephone her daughters whenever she felt the need, no matter where she was.

The chinking of china and hiss of the coffee machine along with Enya's dulcet tones provided background noise, and the yeasty aroma of bread mingled with coffee and cinnamon to make the mouth water.

Maureen paused in her pontificating to crane her neck in order to see whether her scone was being heated. The nautical-themed café served as Maureen's local and they did a lovely scone.

She was feeling the need for butter and lots of it after the stress of Moira's revelation and, given she'd scraped the last of it off the wrapper when she'd made hers and Moira's sandwiches, there'd been nothing else for it but to come down to the village. The baby Kiera's covert Irish dancing lesson would have to wait for another day.

She'd telephoned Rosemary and arranged to meet her here before bundling Kiera into the pram, housed in the spare bedroom for want of a better place to put it.

Donal's eldest daughter Louise had kindly unearthed it from storage for them to have as a spare when Kiera came to visit, and it was coming in very handy indeed.

Nana and granddaughter had had lots of lovely walks already. Maureen enjoyed pointing out all the things of interest in her new neighbourhood to her granddaughter. You saw things with fresh eyes when you'd a baby. Everything from blossoms to daffodils became treasures and worthy of pause to consider.

A BABY AT O'MARA'S

The two squirrels up to the shenanigans in the tree she'd pointed out yesterday had been unfortunate and she wouldn't make that mistake twice. It was only when she'd put her glasses on for a better look, she'd realised the bigger one wasn't giving the littler one a piggyback after all and she'd told Kiera to avert her eyes.

She'd hastily scrawled a note for Moira and Donal to say where they'd gone having left shortly after they did for the driving lesson. She suspected given Moira's temperament, which would try even the most patient of men, they'd be back before she was.

Pooh was jubilant at the prospect of an unexpected walk and he'd trotted alongside Maureen giving excited little yips and yaps as she pushed the pram down the hill towards the village.

It was a surprise to find they'd arrived at the café before Rosemary, given the numerous times they'd been stopped by people, some of whom she knew and some of whom she didn't. Babies and dogs opened a lot of conversational doors, she'd thought to herself, smiling proudly as both were clucked over.

Now, Maureen's gaze flicked over to the window to where she could see Pooh. Rosemary had given him a doggy treat which meant his day was just getting better and better and he was drinking from the bowl of water the café owners left by the lamppost. He'd be happy enough to sit there and watch the world go by while she and Rosemary put the world to rights, she thought, continuing to spout her grievances.

'As the maternal grandmother, I really feel it should be me in charge of the christening, Rosemary.'

'Quite right too, Maureen.'

Two scones were placed in front of them providing a distraction as both women thanked the young lass who'd been helping the fellow who always had a scarf knotted around his head behind the counter.

'Your cappuccinos are on their way.' She smiled and paused to say hello to Kiera. 'Your granddaughter's gorgeous,' she said to Rosemary.

Just like that, Maureen's day went from bad to worse and she barked, 'She's my granddaughter, thank you very much. Can you not see the family resemblance? She has her nana's nose and chin.'

'Erm, yes, of course. Sorry.' The young girl hurried back to the other side of the counter where she'd be safe from the rabid looking little woman.

'I think the baby Kiera needs a wee nap now, don't you, Rosemary?' Maureen suggested in a tone brooking no argument.

Rosemary decided it would be wise not to argue with Maureen especially given she was brandishing a butter knife. She did as she'd been told and settled Kiera down in her pram.

Only when her granddaughter was examining her fingers did Maureen slide the knife through the yellow wedge of butter. It was very symbolic, she thought because Moira choosing Tom's mammy over her was like a knife to the heart. She smeared the butter thickly onto her scone and bit into it.

The cappuccinos arrived next brought to their table by the piratey fellow and as Rosemary stirred a sugar into her cup she said, 'It's a heavy cross to bear alright, Maureen, but I'm sure it will be a grand christening never the less.' She was about to

A BABY AT O'MARA'S

savour her own first bite of fluffy scone when her Nokia began to ring.

Maureen could have sworn Rosemary grew two inches as she straightened importantly and picking up the phone mouthed to Maureen, 'Excuse me, but I'll have to take this. It might be urgent.'

Maureen scowled. What she was really saying was whoever was on that stupid phone of hers was more important than her long-suffering friend. Rosemary did exactly the same thing when she used the call-waiting thingamajig on the landline. It was very annoying so.

'Hello, Fenella,' Rosemary gushed. 'And how was Britney's gymnastics today?'

Fenella was her daughter, Britney her granddaughter who'd a passion for the rhythmic gymnastics.

Maureen eyed her own phone wishing she had an urgent call from one of her daughters to take or, even better, that Roisin would ring to tell her about any accolades Noah had received at school that day but it remained silent. As Rosemary angled away from the table and began chatting in earnest, she remembered she'd planned to call Aisling and, picking the mobile up, hit the speed dial just as Moira had shown her how to do.

'Aisling,' Maureen enunciated loudly and clearly upon hearing her daughter's voice. 'It's me. Your mammy.'

'Why are you shouting, Mammy?'

'Because I'm on the mobile phone in the coffee shop. Can you hear me?'

Jaysus, Aisling thought, Mammy had been the same when she'd spoken to any of their guests who didn't speak English as a first language. She seemed to think the louder she got the easier she was to understand. 'You don't need to shout, I can hear you, Mammy, and so can most of Dublin. Why are you phoning me from a coffee shop and I didn't think you wanted anything to do with that mobile phone?'

'That was before Moira showed me how to use it. Easy-peasy lemon squeezy when you know how. Sure, it's a grand invention. Aren't I here now sipping a cappuccino and talking to you at the same time?'

Aisling silently vowed to swing for her sister when she saw her next. 'Yes, but why are you after telephoning me instead of just enjoying your cappuccino?'

'Because I'm feeling aggrieved so I am and I need your advice as to what to do about it.'

'Mammy, I'm very busy so what is it that has you aggrieved? In ten words or less, go!'

'Moira's after breaking my heart that's what.' Maureen sniffed lowering her voice a notch.

'Again? What's she done now, Mammy?'

Maureen launched into the sorry christening tale oblivious to the two women seated at the table behind her who were as caught up in her family politics as she was.

She finished talking and waited for Aisling to sympathise but instead, she received short shrift. It was the second time that day she'd been told she needed to share her granddaughter she thought, holding the phone away from her ear huffily as Aisling told her off.

'Now listen here, Aisling O'Mara—' she interrupted having had enough.

'It's O'Mara-Moran, Mammy.'

A BABY AT O'MARA'S

'Jaysus wept, she's after telling me what her name is now,' Maureen announced to no one in particular. 'Listen here, Aisling O'Mara-Moran, if I'd wanted your advice, I'd have asked for it.'

'But it was you who rang me and you did ask me for advice in a roundabout way by telling me about the christening arrangements.'

Maureen went very red. 'Don't be bold with me, young lady. I'm ending this call now.' She stabbed at the phone until satisfied she'd turned it off.

Rosemary had disconnected her call too and after telling her old friend about the ungratefulness of her children, she listened with half an ear as Rosemary chattered on about Britney's prowess waving the ribbons about with the pointy toes.

'And have you decided what you'll wear to the christening?' Rosemary asked in an abrupt change of tack a few moments later.

Maureen's mood perked up at the thought of the dress she'd earmarked just the other day for the occasion. Then she remembered she was wanting to lose five pounds before the big day and she gazed regretfully down at her plate upon which not so much as a crumb remained. It was that Sylvia Daly interloper's fault; she'd have to get herself a pair of the tighty-whities, like Bold Brenda to wear under it, she thought mutinously.

'I have as a matter of fact. I called in to see Ciara, she's Ciara with a C not a K like the baby Kiera, you know the girl from the little boutique with the lovely things in the window a few doors down from here?'

'I know it and are you talking about yer wan who looks like she'd snap in a good wind?' Rosemary asked as she scraped the froth from the inside of her cup with her teaspoon.

'Yes, that's her. I've told her she needs to eat but the poor girl's not been blessed with a mammy who feeds her properly which is why I took her a cream bun in when I called in the other day.'

'From Tesco with the fresh cream?'

Maureen nodded, regretting eating the other one she'd bought now too.

'Very good they are too.'

'They are, Rosemary. Although, I think the Tesco bun man's beginning to scrimp a little on the cream.'

A conversation ensued about the sneaky ways of those in the food industry because it transpired Rosemary had counted two slices less in the loaf of bread she favoured. The extra fibre and seeds kept her regular she said, although she spent a fortune in dental floss for getting the little seedy things out of her teeth.

'What were we talking about before?' Maureen asked once they'd exhausted the topic.

'Your dress.'

'Ah yes, well we settled on a bottle green wrap dress because Ciara says the wraps are a very flattering style for women who've borne four children and I've a matching hat with the peacock's feathers in it. She said I'll look a million dollars in it.' It was Maureen's turn to sit a little taller in her chair.

The two women chattered on about who'd been doing what after that until Kiera began to make noises of discontent.

A BABY AT O'MARA'S

Maureen, with a glance at the time, announced she'd best get the wee dote back to her mammy. She hadn't realised they'd been away so long. 'Moira's like a big grizzly bear protecting her cub so she is. She doesn't like letting her out of her sight for long.'

'These young wans think they're the first human beings ever to give birth and raise a child,' Rosemary tutted, swinging her handbag over her shoulder and thrusting her hiking pole forth.

Maureen murmured her agreement following behind Rosemary, hip-a-clicking as she made her way outside into the afternoon sunshine. They said their goodbyes and Pooh wailed plaintively as Rosemary clacked away down the street. It took a few good tugs on his lead to get him moving but the sight of a Bichon Frise strutting her stuff across the way with her owner, who also looked a little like a Bichon Frise, put a spring in his step.

The baby Kiera was proving to be very good for her nana's fitness too, Maureen thought panting as she pushed the pram back up the hill. 'Somebody just walked over my grave, so they did,' she said to Pooh and Kiera with a shiver.

Across town, Aisling was using her mammy's name in vain as glancing at her phone she saw she was pocket calling her for the fourth time that afternoon.

Chapter Fifteen

Donal, who'd nipped into an illegal parking space as close to the guesthouse as he could get, insisted on carting the baby capsule into reception for Moira.

Kiera was once more sound asleep inside it with her head lolling to one side, a plump cheek resting on her shoulder. Her hat had slipped down over one eye too. She'd had a busy afternoon and it was no wonder she was tuckered out.

Moira placed the cottage pie Mammy had pressed into her hands despite her being in the bad books down on the pavement and got the door. She held it open so Donal could pass through before he, in turn, leaned against it so Moira could cart her load in.

The door shut behind them and Moira waved hello while Donal was all smiles as he greeted Aisling and Nina who were in deep conversation behind the front desk. They both looked up on hearing the door open, their faces broadening into smiles seeing Donal with Kiera.

Nina liked Donal; he reminded her of Santa Claus and she was always surprised when he spoke instead of simply, 'Ho, ho, hoing.'

'How're you, ladies?' he asked placing the sleeping baby carefully down on the carpeted floor next to her aunt. 'Dropping off a precious parcel, I am.'

Nina tucked the dark curls that had come loose from her hair bobble behind her ears and smiled down at the sleeping

A BABY AT O'MARA'S

baby. She reminded her of Ana at the same age, she'd the same soft pink flush to her cheeks too. She'd been unable to resist planting a kiss on those cheeks even at the risk of waking her. As much as she'd like to cuddle little Kiera she wouldn't dare wake her though.

'Grand thanks, Donal,' Aisling replied for both of them, her gaze softening as she looked at her sleeping niece. Looking up once more she lowered her voice, 'Well, I say grand. We're grand apart from the guest who's behaving like an arse despite being given the best room in the house.' She jabbed a finger upward and Donal stared at the ceiling as though expecting to see the spectre of the arsey guest.

'He's just given poor Nina here a hard time about the pipes making a noise. We're a quaint Georgian guest house, groaning pipes are par for the course. They add character for goodness sake.'

'Ah,' Donal nodded, rubbing his beard and looking from the Spanish receptionist to his beloved's middle daughter sympathetically. 'Some people would complain about the noise when opportunity knocks so they would.'

Aisling agreed with him, staring hard at her mammy's live-in man friend.

Nina played this saying over in her mind trying to make sense of it and when she finally did she decided it was a very wise thing to have said indeed. These Irish said some very odd things at times but sometimes they made perfect sense too.

'You're looking a tad pale on it there, Donal. You're not coming down with something are you?' Aisling asked.

'No, no, I'm as fit as a fiddle, Aisling. Now, I best be off before I get another, erm, ticket.'

Moira was lurking behind him and he jumped as he turned to leave to find her blocking his way.

'Thanks a million for dropping me and Kiera home, Donal, and for this afternoon. It was a great craic.' She beamed.

'Yer welcome, there, Moira.'

'Would you take me out again for another driving lesson?'

Donal had the look of a cornered animal and Aisling nudged Nina, whispering, 'That's why he looks like he's suffering from the shock.'

'Erm,' the hesitancy was clear on Donal's face.

'Please, Donal. I'm sorry about the ticket. I'll fix you up for it and I won't mix the accelerator up with the brake again. Mammy's always after saying I learn things the hard way.'

Ticket aside, Moira felt the driving lesson had gone well on the whole. Donal made a very good instructor and she'd been grand once the country music had settled her nerves down.

Donal scratched his beard. Moira had been the hardest O'Mara child to win over when he'd begun to step out with Maureen and, despite fearing for his life on several occasions and receiving a hefty fine, he'd enjoyed getting to know Mo's youngest daughter better today.

'There's no need to sort me out for anything and, of course, I'll give you another lesson, Moira. We'll have you mobile in no time,' he found himself saying against his better judgment. He'd be sure to have a stack of relaxing country music hits to hand when he next took her out because she had settled down once he'd put the CD on. As for his nerves, sure they'd be fine once he got a glass of red into him. Actually, he thought, he might make it something stiffer like a shot of whiskey. Yes, a spot of Kenny and a nip of the hard stuff and he'd be right as rain.

A BABY AT O'MARA'S

'Oh, and, Donal, don't breathe a word of the you know what thing to Mammy will you. I'll never hear the end of it if you do.'

'I won't say a word, Moira.'

She stepped out of his way and Donal pretended to doff his cap. 'I'll be on my way then, ladies. I want to beat the rush hour.'

'Fair play to you. The traffic's getting terrible so it is,' Aisling remarked.

'That it is and good luck with him upstairs. Bye now.' He disappeared out the door with a final wave to them all.

'Breathe a word of what you know what thing?' Aisling's ears had been burning.

'None of your business,' Moira snapped. There was the ticket, of course. She didn't want Mammy hearing about that, but there was no way she was letting any member of her family know that when Donal had slipped the mellow country music CD into the player, she'd relaxed behind the wheel. They'd never let her hear the end of it, and Aisling would have a whale of a time suggesting she become a backup singer for The Gamblers or that she should join Mammy's line dancing group.

'How're you, Nina?' Moira directed her attention to their Spanish receptionist. She'd always felt there was more to Nina than met the eye but despite them being friendly with one another Nina had never let her guard down.

Nina smiled. 'I am fine, Moira. The restaurant was very busy today. I'm glad to be sitting down, oh and I bought this.' She leaned over and retrieved her backpack from under the desk opening it to show Moira the coloured rings she'd bought for Kiera from Mothercare. 'They're for Kiera to play with when I look after her.'

Moira was touched. 'She'll love those.'

Nina looked pleased as she put them away once more before asking, 'How was your day?'

Moira was unsure how to answer. It had certainly been action-packed, what with the mammy-coffee group, the mobile phone lessons, and the driving lesson. Put the broken nights of sleep into the mix and it was all beginning to catch up with her. She felt as though she could sleep for a week.

'It's been busy too.'

Aisling remembered she'd a bone to pick with her sister. 'Oi, you. What were you thinking, teaching Mammy to use the mobile phone? She pocket-called me seven times this afternoon I'll have you know!'

Moira grinned. 'Sorry but I want her to know how to use it so as I can ring her from college and check in on Kiera. She's on about taking her to feed the ducks and that sorta thing. I won't be able to concentrate if I can't get hold of her and I deserve a medal for my efforts. I'm surprised my hair didn't spontaneously turn white with the stress of it. She's not an easy woman to teach.'

Aisling shook her head slowly, the gold in her reddish, blonde hair glinting under the light. 'I don't think you fully grasp what you've done. You've unleashed a monster, Moira, we are contactable by Mammy at all times. Did you think about that?'

On cue, Moira's phone began to ring. She fumbled about in the baby bag for it.

'Hello?'

A BABY AT O'MARA'S

'Moira, it's me your mammy.'

'Feck.'

'Moira, you're not after swearing in front of the baby Kiera, I hope.'

'No, Mammy, I'm in reception and Aisling's taken Kiera upstairs.'

Aisling smirked and mouthed, 'Told you so,' before picking the capsule up and taking her niece upstairs.

Moira watched her go wistfully wishing she'd not answered now. 'Why are you shouting, Mammy?'

'Because I'm in the garden on the mobile.'

'But I can hear you perfectly well. You'll give me earache bellowing like that.'

'Oh, and you've never given me the earache, have you?'

Moira fidgeted, eager to head upstairs in case Tom was already home. She wanted to tell him all about her day. She supposed she should be grateful her mammy was talking to her at all and as such, she decided to be nice.

'And what is it you were wanting then, Mammy?'

'Is Donal on his way home? Only it's warm enough to sit in the garden and I thought I'd do us some cheese and tomato crackers to have with our afternoon tipple and I don't want them going soggy.' Maureen intended to make the most of her garden with its sea view now the warmer weather was coming and sitting in the garden for an evening drink and nibbles seemed a very civilised thing to do.

'He's not long left, Mammy.'

'Grand. Oh, and, Moira...'

'Yes, Mammy?'

'I've taken it upon myself to write out a list of who you need to invite to the christening on the O'Mara side. I'll not have it on my head if you forget to send an invitation to your second cousin Sheridan or my aunt Dolly.'

Moira had heard of neither of these people. 'Who're they when they're at home? And I don't recall them being at Rosi's or Ash's weddings so how come you're wanting me to invite them to Kiera's christening?'

'They were both there at both weddings, Moira, you were too busy groping Tom at Aisling's wedding to notice and at Roisin's you'd your eye on Colin—'

'The chinless feck,' Moira added automatically.

'Your sister's ex-husband's,' Maureen said primly, 'cousin.'

It was true enough he'd been a fine thing so he had. Unfortunately for her, he'd also been gay. She'd realised this when she'd busted out her sexy Beyoncé moves on the dance floor and he'd not batted an eye.

Now, Moira tuned out her mammy who'd managed to dredge up numerous other long-lost relatives by the sound of things, none of whom could possibly be left off the invitation list for fear of family feuding. The christening was going to be on a par with the papal inauguration at this rate.

'I hope you're jotting them all down, Moira.'

Moira didn't say anything. She wasn't.

'Get a pen and paper,' Maureen ordered.

Moira knew that tone of voice and she knew better than to argue. She retrieved both from the reception desk leaning on the top as she said, 'Right, I'm ready. Read them out then.'

Her fingers were cramping by the time she'd finished writing down a list that was like a who's who of Ireland.

A BABY AT O'MARA'S

'And would you like me to send the invitations out when you have them to hand given I've got where everybody lives written down in my address book or is Tom's mammy going to be doing that too?'

Moira rubbed her temple with her spare hand. She'd had enough. 'If you could send them out once the invitations are printed that would be very helpful, Mammy. Now I've got to go, I need the loo.'

'You've a mobile haven't you?'

'What's that got to do with it?'

'Take it with you, I won't listen.'

'Jaysus wept, Mammy, I'm hanging up now and don't be ringing me back.'

Moira rolled her eyes at Nina as she shoved her phone in her pocket and received a sympathetic smile in return; she could imagine what her mother would be like if she had a mobile phone.

Moira said goodnight to Nina and took to the stairs. Aisling was right, she thought, thundering up them, she had unleashed a monster.

Chapter Sixteen

The scent of frying onions and garlic along with something else she couldn't put a finger on was a salve on Moira's mood as she stepped inside the apartment. She forgot about her annoying conversation with Mammy as she closed the door behind her and sniffed her way through to the living room.

Aisling was curled up on the sofa with Kiera in her arms having an in-depth conversation with her niece as to the soap on the tele. It was *Emmerdale*, the long-running Yorkshire-set drama revolving around life in the small village of the same name.

Moira watched in disbelief as her sister pointed to the screen and said, 'Look, Kiera, that's the Woolpack pub and that man there, he's Eric Pollard, he's a baddie so he is.'

'Are you brainwashing my daughter with *Emmerdale*? You'll be telling her to "put t'kettle on" next.' Moira said in a dodgy Yorkshire accent.

'It's better than *Fair City*,' Aisling shot back, although she was apt to stare goggle-eyed at the screen when the Dublin serial was on too.

Moira opened her mouth to debate the point but shut it again in favour of dumping the baby bag and making her way into the kitchen to see what Tom was cooking up.

He grinned at her, wooden spoon in hand. 'How're you?'

'Grand now.' Moira wrapped her arms around him and rested her head for a moment on his chest enjoying the solidness of it. She angled her head up for a kiss which he planted on her before disentangling himself.

'The onions will burn if I don't turn the heat down.'

'It smells gorgeous. What're you making?'

'Spag bol, my specialty.'

'My favourite,' Moira stated loyally, watching as he tipped the mince in the pan and began to break it up with the spoon. She stifled a yawn and opened the cupboard where the pans were stacked and hefted out the pasta pot.

'So, how did the coffee morning go?' Tom asked not looking up from his task.

Moira filled him in, skimming over the way she'd felt like a sub-standard mammy because she'd not been able to breastfeed. Tom would tell her she was being silly and overly sensitive which she probably was but she couldn't help how she felt and she didn't want him jollying her along.

'Cliona was a pain in the arse. Mrs Perfect. The rest of us all looked like your regular mammies about town but she could have been doing a photoshoot for *HELLO!* magazine. But I did meet two mammies, Mona and Lisa...' Tom's snigger saw her voice trail off. 'What?' she asked eyeing him as she filled the pasta pot with hot water.

'Mona Lisa.'

'Tom, that's not even funny.' Moira shook her head but she couldn't help but smile. 'Anyway, they were a good craic.'

'That's great.' He looked pleased as he began adding the tinned tomatoes and paste to his brew while Moira grabbed a spaghetti noodle and chomped into it.

'Can you hear her?' She tilted her head toward Aisling in the living room. 'She's after talking to Kiera in a Yorkshire accent now. You do realise by the time our families are done we're going to have an Irish dancing, Yorkshire accented, bilingual child.'

'Well, she's bound to be talented with us for parents although your mammy's pushing her luck with the Irish dancing. I've two left feet.' Tom laughed, doing a little jig to demonstrate his point and then seeing what Moira was doing grimaced, 'That's disgusting you know.'

It was rather but the end of the noodle disappeared into her mouth nevertheless and when she'd swallowed it down Moira said, 'I can't help it. Since I had Kiera I'll eat anything. It's been a busy day actually. Donal took me for a driving lesson today.'

'Good man.' Tom was all ears as she told him what had transpired on the back roads of Dublin earlier that afternoon. Silently he thought Donal a much braver man than he.

'Jaysus, Moira.' He shook his head when she reached the part where the gardai had given chase. 'There's never a dull moment when you're around but at least you were safe.'

'Ah, but it's worked out in the end, Tom, because...' Moira shot a glance over at her sister to make sure she wasn't earwigging. 'I've a secret driving weapon.'

'Oh yes, and what would that be?'

'The country music,' Moira whispered explaining how it had miraculously calmed her fractious nerves and ensured the rest of the lesson went swimmingly. 'I was getting the hang of it and Donal's promised me he'll take me out again.'

The man should be up for a bravery award, Tom thought, sprinkling basil over the meaty sauce as he shook his head.

'What did Mammy want earlier?' Aisling called over.

A BABY AT O'MARA'S

'She wanted to know if Donal had left to head home but you know Mammy she couldn't just ask that and then get off the phone. She was going on about long-lost relatives I've to invite to the christening. I think she made them up because I've never heard of them.' She decided not to mention how the news Tom's mammy, Sylvia, would be helping with the christening arrangements had gone down like a lead balloon in front of him. 'I had to tell her I was desperate for the loo to get her off the fecking thing in the end and do you know what she said?'

'What?' Aisling asked, somehow knowing she wouldn't be surprised by whatever it was.

'She said I should take the phone into the toilet with me because that was the whole point of having a mobile phone. You can take it anywhere.'

Aisling laughed and then sobered. 'Ah Jaysus, I told you. She'll drive us demented so she will. And I wouldn't put it past her to ring us while she's sitting on the throne either just because she can.'

'Did I miss something?' Tom asked sampling the sauce and then adding a splash of red wine.

'Moira's after teaching Mammy how to use the mobile phone Donal bought her.'

Tom raised an eyebrow, his mouth turned up at the corner.

'I wouldn't be looking so amused if I were you,' Moira said to him. 'She's got your number on the speed dial too.'

He made a note to self to make sure his phone was switched off when he was in lectures.

'I wanted to be able to get hold of her when I'm at college but...' Moira lowered her voice once more not wanting to give Aisling any further leverage. 'I think it was a mistake.'

'Moira, your mammy raised four children. She's perfectly capable of looking after Kiera without you phoning in every hour. We've had that conversation.'

'I know and I know but I feel strange about leaving her. I can't help it, Tom.'

Tom kissed her on the tip of her nose. 'It's natural but you'll both be grand. Sure, you're leaving her with family. You know the saying about it taking a village to raise a child.'

Moira frowned not quite getting his point. 'And Nina don't forget, she's on board too.'

'And Nina,' he agreed. 'Has she younger siblings back home?'

Moira shrugged. 'Not that she's ever mentioned.' Nina hadn't told them much about her life in Spain, she realised. 'But she did say she's used to being around babies and Aisling will be around if she needs her. She's lovely with Kiera too. She's bought her a set of coloured rings to play with when she looks after her.'

'That's kind of her. I have to say though she always seems a little sad to me.'

So, it wasn't just her being fanciful then because she often thought the same. Not for the first time, Moira wondered what Nina's story was.

The water in the pot was beginning to bubble and Moira called over her shoulder. 'Oi Annie Sugden over there, are you having your dinner with us or are you heading off to Quinn's?'

A BABY AT O'MARA'S

'I'm eating with you and then I'm going over to see Leila. We haven't caught up in ages because she spends all her time with her Bearach these days. Between you and me, I think she's not far off from making an announcement where he's concerned. They've gotten very serious of late.'

There were telling signs like the fact her friend couldn't say a sentence without his name popping up in it. It would be nice for Leila, who spent her days coordinating other couple's weddings, to have her own big day. It would also be nice for Moira and Tom to have some time to themselves this evening given Tom wasn't working which was another reason why she was making herself scarce.

'I'm looking forward to it. We're having a girly evening in with a movie.'

'Bearach that's an unusual name,' Tom said.

'It means Barry,' Aisling informed him. 'Personally, I don't know which one's worse. Do you Leila take thee Barry or do you Leila take thee Bearach?'

Moira laughed as she dropped the appropriate handful of spaghetti into the water. 'Oh, Ash, while I think of it, do you remember a second cousin Sheridan and Great Aunt Dolly. Mammy says they were at both yours and Rosi's weddings.'

Aisling frowned. 'Yes, no wait that was Suzanne, not Sheridan. There's so many of them that crawl out the woodwork when it comes to weddings and funerals but no, those names don't sound familiar. Why?'

'Oh, Mammy was on about them being invited to the christening only I've never heard of them either.'

'Like I said we're like one of those Appalachian mountain families in America where everybody's related. They all leave their cabins and come down from the hills when they catch wind of a family function where there's to be free grog and food.'

'She's joking, Tom,' Moira said, seeing his alarmed expression. Well, half joking at any rate she thought to herself.

'That reminds me,' Tom said leaving the Bolognese to simmer. 'My mam was after ringing earlier; she wanted to know how you were placed to catch up with her tomorrow to run through the plans for the christening.'

Moira bit down on her lip to stop a retort bursting forth she'd regret. She was fed up with hearing about the fecking thing. She glanced over at Kiera feeling bad. It was her day, not Moira's and it would all work out in the end she knew. Maybe she should phone Rosi after tea and get her to run through some of that calm down yoga breathing. It couldn't do any harm.

'Moira?'

'Sorry, yeah sure, that'll be grand.'

'Will you give her a ring then and let her know after dinner?'

Moira nodded and busied herself fetching plates. She didn't want Tom to know she was anxious about spending one on one time with his mam. They didn't know each other at all really but they both thought the world of the same man; surely that had to count for something.

Kiera was happy to stretch out under her baby gym and bat at the stuffed toys dangling down while the trio sat down for their dinner.

There wasn't much chatter between the slurping of noodles and they'd all the tell-tale orange rim around their mouths

A BABY AT O'MARA'S

from the sauce by the time they'd forked and twirled the last of the pasta.

'That was delicious, Tom, thank you,' Aisling said, getting up and gathering the dishes. 'I'll clean up and then I'll leave you both to it.'

'Glad you enjoyed it, Aisling,' Tom said, getting up from the table oblivious to the blob of sauce on the end of his nose. He was pleased Aisling had volunteered her services in the kitchen because he was a messy cook and he was also shattered.

He lay down on the floor next to Kiera, hoping he didn't nod off because he wanted to be the one to bathe her before they put her down for the night. Or, at least until she needed her eleven o'clock feed.

Moira stayed at the table and her gaze was soft as she watched Tom and Kiera. Sometimes she could pinch herself as to how it had worked out for them.

Hats off to Mammy for that one. Sometimes her interfering paid off because if she hadn't gone round to talk to Tom and got to the bottom of why he'd reacted the way he had to Moira's unexpected pregnancy news, she might have been raising Kiera on her own. Looking at the pair of them now, she couldn't imagine what it would be like for him not to be a part of their life.

Moira resolved to focus on how lucky she was. She'd set all those other insecurities aside she thought, biting her nail, another habit she'd undertaken of late. If Rosi were here she'd tell her to be mindful of the blessings in her life. She could be very annoying with all her new age ideas at times could Rosi but there were times too when she could be wise. She'd give her a call tonight, she decided, but first things first she needed to ring Sylvia.

Aisling was clattering about in the kitchen so she took the phone, into their bedroom and made the call. A brief chat with Tom's dad, whom she liked immensely, ensued and then he put Sylvia on.

'Thanks for ringing me back, Moira. I won't keep you long,' the no-nonsense Mrs Daly said and upon hearing Moira was free the next day asked, 'Would it suit you if I dropped in around tenish?'

Moira was about to say that would be grand when Sylvia carried on.

'Or, if you wanted to get out and about I could pick you up and we could go for coffee and a bite to eat. There's a lovely little café I know over in Castleknock Village. The food's gorgeous and if you need to pick anything up there's plenty of shops there. Oh, and there's a wonderful boutique baby and childrenswear shop in the village too. I wondered whether we might have a look at a christening gown for Kiera while we're there?'

She sounded excited, Moira thought, not wanting to dampen her enthusiasm by saying she'd rather not troop around the shops and that she and Tom weren't in the position to be spending money at expensive baby boutiques. She'd much rather stay home and have Sylvia watch Kiera for an hour or so as she could get her head down once they'd chatted through all things christening.

Instead of saying this, however, she injected a bright and breezy enthusiasm she didn't feel at the prospect and said, 'I'd love to head out. Thank you, Sylvia, that sounds like a good plan. I'll be ready for tenish. I'll come out so as you don't have to park.'

As she said her goodbyes, she marvelled at the difference between Sylvia and Mammy. Sylvia had managed to get straight to the point of their call and make arrangements in under sixty seconds whereas Mammy would have gotten so off track she'd have forgotten what it was they were supposed to be organising in the first place. Tom was right, it would be a good opportunity to get to know her daughter's other nana better.

When she wandered back into the living room she saw Tom's eyes were shut and his mouth was slack. He'd be dribbling any minute now she thought, shaking her head. How he could sleep with Aisling banging about in the kitchen she didn't know. Well, she did actually. When you were *that* tired you could sleep through anything.

'I would say enjoy your evening but I've got a feeling you won't be up to much other than sleeping,' Aisling said.

The very thought of stretching out in bed was bliss but first, Moira thought, she'd another phone call to make.

Chapter Seventeen

Moira smiled as she swung her legs onto the sofa, phone in hand. She could hear Tom's voice over the running taps in the bathroom as he chatted to Kiera about his day. This was his special time with his daughter and he'd follow it up by giving her a bottle before settling her down in the cot they'd set up in the corner of their bedroom. He'd pull the cord of her Humpty Dumpty mobile and watch her for a few moments before tiptoeing out of the room. His routine with her on the nights he wasn't working was precious.

Kiera didn't like being left and she'd protest loudly when she realised she was alone and Daddy wasn't going to pull the cord on Humpty again. It wouldn't last long though because, despite her best efforts, sleep would overcome her tiny body.

Moira had learned the hard way not to keep going in and trying to settle her when she cried. It only made things worse as Kiera would get overstimulated and Moira overwrought. It was hard to listen to her wails though. They tugged at her, calling her in.

The first week after they'd brought her home from hospital she'd thought she'd heard Kiera crying even when she wasn't. The sound got trapped inside your head but then it was designed to, she supposed.

Hopefully tonight, she'd snooze for a good stretch before she woke for her next feed. She and Tom could both hit the hay then. The thought of uninterrupted sleep was bliss.

A BABY AT O'MARA'S

Aisling had gone off to get changed before she headed around to Leila's and, knowing she'd half an hour or so before she'd want to be climbing into bed, she rang Rosi. Her sister picked up after a few rings.

'Hello, Roisin speaking,' she sounded breathless.

'Hi, Rosi speaking, it's your sister.' Moira couldn't resist. It had always irritated her when friends of her mammy's and daddy's would reply with this when she answered the phone as she'd been taught to do as a child.

'Very funny, Moira.'

'Why are you all out of breath?' Moira frowned. 'You've not got Shay over there with you have you?' Those two were like rabbits when they got together. A stab of envy shot through her. She was far too tired for doing any hopping about with Tom.

'Chance would be a fine thing. No, he's coming to stay next weekend and I can't wait to see him. It feels like ages since I saw him last.'

The foundations of Rosi's flat over there in London would be rocking then, Moira thought, guessing it would be Noah's weekend to stay with his dad.

'And I'm out of breath because it's been mad here and I only got back in the door five minutes ago.'

Moira was disappointed; she was in the mood to chat. 'Do you want me to call you back tomorrow then?'

'No, you're grand. You get very good at the multitasking once you're a mammy, Moira, as you'll find out. I'll heat up some sausage and beans for our dinner and talk to you at the same time.' As if to prove her point there was the sound of cupboard doors opening and closing.

'Mummy, what's for tea?' A voice sounded in the background.

'How're you, Noah,' Moira called.

'Your aunty Moira's on the phone, she says hello,' Roisin said.

'Hello, Aunty Moira. Mummy, what's for tea?' he whined.

Tired, poor love, Moira surmised.

'Beans on toast, now off you go and cheer Mr Nibbles up. 'G'wan with you.'

'You sounded just like Mammy then. It was spooky.'

'I tell you, Moira, children have a sixth sense as to when you're wanting a grown-up conversation.'

Moira laughed as she heard her nephew chanting gaily, 'Baked beans are good for your heart, baked beans will make you fart.'

'Noah, cut that out,' Roisin called after him. 'Sorry about that. He thinks anything to do with letting off is hilarious at the moment. He's terrible when he goes to visit Granny Quealey, what with her having reached the age where she breaks wind every time she bends over.'

'I don't blame him, I'd giggle too,' Moira said. She was thoughtful for a moment. 'Rosi, what's with the things that pop out of your mouth of their own accord once you become a parent? I was after telling Tom to close the door because he wasn't born in a barn the other day and he's been saying all sorts of Mammyish things too.'

'It gets worse, Moira. I found myself saying to Noah, "I suppose you think those socks will pick themselves up," last night.'

'No! That was a Mammy special.'

A BABY AT O'MARA'S

'I know. Can you imagine when he's a teenager?'

Moira sniggered and she put on her best Maureen O'Mara voice, 'If so and so's mammy let them jump off a cliff, would you want me to let you do it too? Or, when you have your own house then you can make the rules.'

The sisters giggled then Roisin piped up, 'Jaysus wept, Moira, it's only a matter of time. You wait, you've a daughter. You'll be asking her, 'Where do you think yer going in that get-up?'

'Ah no.'

'It's inevitable. And how is my beautiful niece?'

'She's grand.'

'And Tom?'

'He's tired but grand he's giving her a bath now.'

'He's a good man, Moira. I'm so pleased it worked out for you. Colin was never hands-on like that with Noah when he was a baby.'

'That's because he was a chinless feck.'

Roisin laughed. 'And you?'

'Oh, Rosi...' Moira poured it all out, her eyes smarting with tired tears as she told her big sister how some days she felt as if her head was barely above water and that out of a score of one to ten in a mammy test, she'd score a four-point five on a good day.

Roisin cut her off when she told her about the coffee morning and how Cliona and most of the other mammies there had it all under control so, why did she feel like she had no control whatsoever?

'Listen to me, Moira O'Mara,' she said sternly. 'You've a baby who's only just over a month old. Be kind to yourself and do not, do you hear me, do not compare yourself to others. That's a miserable way to live your life so it is. As for that Cliona, her type always manages to appear when you're at a low ebb, but none of us knows what goes on behind closed doors, and her life is probably nowhere near as perfect as she'd have you think.'

'Mammy said something along those lines too but I'm not so sure, Rosi, it did look pretty perfect.' Moira flashed back to all those soft lilac hues and the calm atmosphere. 'She'd baked and she'd a full face of makeup on.'

Roisin ignored her. 'And, feeling inadequate is normal. Sure, I was the same. I remember thinking if I bought a tin of the baby food instead of making it from scratch I was letting Noah down. I don't know why we women do it but we seem to set ourselves these impossibly high standards. Take some advice from someone who has been where you are now and lower the bar a little, Moira. You'll be a far better mammy for it.'

Moira soaked up what her sister was saying, trying to take it all on board. 'And would you prescribe some bendy yoga breathing exercises too?'

'I would. The pranayama will help. It literally means to extend the life force.'

'Rosi, I don't need all the ins and outs just tell me how to do the pranyamy.'

'Pranayama. I'll run through it with you now so lie down on the floor with your knees bent about hip-width apart.'

'Wait, I'm getting on the floor now.' Moira arranged herself as her sister was instructing, phone pressed to her ear. 'Okay, I'm on my back, what's next?'

A BABY AT O'MARA'S

'Place your palm on your tummy and just become aware of your breath. Observe the quality of it—'

'Rosi, why are you speaking all funny like that?'

'Don't interrupt, Moira. And I'm not speaking funny.'

'You are.'

'That's how you're supposed to speak when you're teaching yoga.'

'It's a little bit creepy to be honest, Rosi. You sound like a voiceover for a scary film. You know like *Friday the 13th*. God, yer Jason wan gave me the holy terrors so he did.'

'Moira, do you want me to help you or not?'

'I do, I really do.'

'Stop interrupting then and get back to yer breathing.'

That was much more like the Rosi she knew and loved, Moira thought, concentrating on her inhaling and exhaling once more.

'Okay, so now let your breathing become relaxed, slow and steady, slow and steady.'

Moira felt her tummy gently rising and descending and the tension floated from her shoulders as she relaxed.

'Now, I want you to take a moment, a pause at the end of each in-breath and out-breath. Feel how your tummy naturally expands with each inhalation and the contraction as you exhale.' Roisin was silent for a few beats while Moira sank deeper into her breathing. 'Gently increase the inhalation so as your diaphragm expands and feel how it contracts as you slow your exhalation. You're giving yourself the opportunity to enjoy a full, relaxed breath.'

Moira was beginning to feel like she could drift off. Her body felt soft and light, floaty almost.

'I'm going to open the can of sausage and beans now,' Roisin said in that same soothing, voice, 'I want you to continue the practice for at least six more full breaths.'

Moira was vaguely aware of a thump as Roisin put the phone down on the worktop. She carried on with her rhythmic breathing.

'Moira!'

'What?' Moira blinked her eyes open started by the tinny, bellow coming from the phone. It was lying on the floor near her head. She had nodded off she realised picking it up once more. 'I must have dropped off, sorry, Rosi.'

'Don't be sorry, you were supposed to be relaxed. How do you feel?'

Moira took a moment to examine herself mentally. 'Actually, I think it helped.'

'It will. Breathing like that calms your nervous system and it helps with stress and anxiety. Practise it whenever you get the chance.'

'I think you're going to be a grand yoga teacher, Rosi. But I think you might need to work on the voice.' Her sister had dreams of opening her own yoga studio one day.

'There's nothing wrong with my voice.' Roisin huffed.

'If you say so.' Moira was feeling too serene to get into a debate. She remembered Roisin's harried tone when she'd picked up the phone. 'So come on then, what had you flapping so?'

There was a hissing sigh down the line. 'Mr fecking Nibbles is what's been happening. The stress of it all, Moira. Honestly, that gerbil's harder work than Noah.'

A BABY AT O'MARA'S

'Is he alright?' Moira asked with a sinking heart at her sister's tone. She knew how much her nephew loved his pet gerbil.

'He's lucky to be alive, put it that way because I was tempted so I was.'

'What happened?'

'Noah and I arrived home this evening to find him lying on his back with his little gerbil legs sticking up in the air. His tongue was lolling out to one side. It was horrible so it was.'

'Ah Jaysus, what a thing. Did you perform the mouth to mouth?'

'No, I did not. Noah announced he was still warm and I did think about doing the one finger CPR but I decided it might be safer to get him to the vet which was why we were stuck in the rush hour traffic for an hour. It was the longest hour of my life what with Noah's crying and Mr Nibbles twitching.'

'Was it the epilepsy then? Had he had a seizure?'

'No, yer vet man charged me an arm and a leg to tell us Mr Nibbles is in fine fettle physically. Emotionally however he's a wreck. Playing dead was a cry for help and I haven't a clue what the twitching was in aid of.'

'I don't understand?'

'Mr Nibbles is depressed.'

Moira snorted. 'Sure, he lives the life of Riley that one, what with all those lovely salad greens and that wheel of his, what's he got to get all maudlin about?'

'He's lonely. He doesn't like being on his own. Apparently, the best thing we can do for him is find him a friend.'

'A Mrs Nibbles?'

'No, I'm not having that going on under my roof, thank you very much.'

A tad hypocritical on her sister's part, Moira thought.

'I'm going to ring Colin after tea seeing as it was him who gave Noah, Mr Nibbles in the first place and tell him he's to pay half the vet bill and find a suitable friend to keep him company while Noah and I are out during the day.'

'Good for you, Rosi.'

'Do you ever wonder what the little sausages are made of in the beans?'

'No, and I wouldn't think about it too hard if I were you either,' Moira said.

'You're probably right. I know why you're ringing.'

'Do you?'

'Yes, Mammy rang when we were sitting in the waiting room. It was hard to hear her over the noise the budgie and the cat were making but I got the gist of what she was on about. You've asked Tom's mam to help you organise the christening.'

This time it was Moira's sigh that was weighty. 'I can imagine what she said. To be honest, Rosi, I'd rather nobody was helping me organise it. If it were up to me, I'd just have a small ceremony for immediate family and close friends. I mean have you ever heard of a second cousin called Sheridan or a Great Aunt Dolly?'

'They're not ringing any bells.'

'Mammy's after saying they were at yours and Aisling's weddings but she's no clue who they are either. So why the feck should I invite these relatives none of us have heard of to my daughter's christening?' Her voice had risen a notch and she heard Tom call out.

A BABY AT O'MARA'S

'You okay there, Moira?'

'Grand, just chatting to Rosi,' she called back.

'Because that's what you do, Moira. Sure when I married Colin I felt like I was juggling eggs trying to keep his mam and our mammy happy. The christening was the same. Sometimes it's just easier to go with the flow. You'll learn to pick your battles. It's one day and it means a lot to the mammies so grit your teeth and send out the invitations to Sheridan and Great Aunt Dolly.'

'You just gave me a modernised version of the Serenity Prayer.'

Rosi laughed. 'I suppose I did. They're wise words though, Moira.'

Moira studied her chewed fingernail. Rosi was right, she decided. She'd grit her teeth and get on with it. It was silly to waste her precious little energy on worrying over it.

'I'm going to have to go in a sec the beans are beginning to bubble.'

'Well before you go, guess what?'

'What?'

'I had a driving lesson with Donal today.'

'Good for you! How did it go.'

'Well apart from the gardai giving chase, it went well.'

'Jaysus, Moira, there's never a dull moment with you.' Roisin repeated Tom's earlier remark.

Moira jumped as Aisling suddenly bellowed by her ear. She hadn't heard her come back in the room. 'Do you know, she's only after teaching Mammy how to use her mobile phone. It's a nightmare so it is.'

'Don't worry, Rosi,' Moira said sitting up. 'She won't want to pay the charges for ringing you. You and Pat will be safe.'

Aisling stuck her tongue out at her sister. Moira raised her middle finger as Tom walked back into the room with Kiera. He looked bemusedly at the sisters.

'Hello, Rosi,' he called out.

'Shite the beans are sticking to the pan.' Rosi hung up.

Tom placed Kiera, who looked particularly delicious in her teddy bear patterned sleepsuit, in Moira's arms and she breathed in the soft lavender scent of her.

'I'll just make up her bottle,' he said. 'How's Rosi?'

Aisling perched on the arm of the sofa and was gazing adoringly at her niece as Moira filled them both in on the Mr Nibbles drama.

As her sister crossed her legs, Moira noticed the flash of hot pink on her feet. She took a closer look.

Louboutin's, she gasped silently noting the telltale, signature red sole and impossibly high heel. They were gorgeous. God she couldn't imagine stalking about in a pair of them these days. 'Are they new?' Moira asked inclining her head towards the glossy leather.

'These old things?' Aisling said, feigning innocence as she glanced over her shoulder as though expecting Quinn to suddenly rear up.

'Ash, it's me. I won't threaten to snip the credit card in half. Besides, I know every pair of designer shoes you own intimately and those have never graced my feet.'

Aisling looked sheepish. 'Yes, they're new. I couldn't resist them. It's the endorphin rush when I watch the sales assistant put them in that brown box and slide them across the counter

A BABY AT O'MARA'S

toward me. It's addictive. Quinn doesn't understand. It's a girl thing.'

Moira glanced down at Kiera, who was beginning to wriggle in anticipation of her bottle which her daddy was currently testing on his wrist, then back at her sister. She knew Aisling would gladly throw all her expensive shoes out the window and walk around in wooden clogs for the rest of her days if she could have a baby of her own. She also knew Aisling turned into a shopaholic when she was stressed.

She wasn't as vocal about her and Quinn trying for a baby as she had been. In fact, she'd gone very quiet on the subject and seemed to be more relaxed about it all now but Moira wasn't fooled. She watched her with Kiera and the longing on her face was plain to see. She hoped it happened soon for her sister.

Tom came over and took Kiera from Moira; he'd feed her in the peace of their bedroom. He glanced down at the topic of their conversation and shook his head. 'I don't know how you girls manage to get about in shoes like that.'

'We don't have a choice, Tom,' Aisling said twirling her ankle to admire the sheen of pink. 'Not if we don't want to spend our entire lives looking up other people's nostrils. You try being short.'

He laughed. 'Right, time for this wee girl to get to bed.'

'I'll be in in a minute,' Moira said. 'Aisling, do not kiss her; you've lipstick on brighter than your shoes. People already think the child's got a lip-shaped birthmark on her forehead.'

Aisling had to content herself with a wave and a 'Night, night, sweetheart.' She got up from the sofa and announced she'd be off.

'Why're you so dressed up if you're only watching a movie at Leila's.'

'Because I have standards, Moira, and I want to show her my new shoes.' Aisling skipped from the room and Moira glanced ruefully down at her pilled socks.

Her standards had gone out the window and, heaving herself off the sofa, she padded to the bedroom.

Chapter Eighteen

🍵

Moira scooted over to the far side of the plush cream sofa with its green stripes in the reception area of the guesthouse. She fidgeted for a moment or two before stretching over its rolled arm so as she could peer out the window to the street beyond once more.

'Moira, come away from the window. You'll be frightening the passers-by staring out at them like so. It's only quarter to ten and from what you said about her, Tom's mammy sounds like a punctual woman,' Bronagh bossed as she paced the carpeted entrance with Kiera cradled in her arms. She was in her element.

To Bronagh's utter delight, Kiera had been awake when Moira had appeared five minutes earlier and she'd wasted no time in whipping her out of that contraption she was strapped into for a cuddle. Even better, there was no chance of Mrs Flaherty muscling in on the act either because Bronagh knew Aisling was currently down in the kitchen smoothing the cook's ruffled feathers. The little red fox had paid a visit to the bins the night before, something Moira confirmed upon hearing this.

She'd been settling Kiera back down in her cot shortly after eleven when she'd heard the distant clatter of the bin lid being toppled. It was a sound as familiar as the groaning pipes of the guesthouse and she'd tiptoed across to the window silently. A thin veil of condensation had to be wiped away before she could squint down below. The sensor light had flicked on and she was in time to spy him slinking across the courtyard. Quick as a flash, he flattened himself down and disappeared back through the hole under the brick wall that separated the guesthouse from the Iveagh Gardens.

Moira hoped he'd taken a tasty piece of bacon, sausage or black pudding back with him.

Foxy Loxy as Moira called him wasn't the only reason Mrs Flaherty was blustering this morning though, Bronagh informed her. Mr McNulty in Room 8 had complained his bacon was erring on the side of burnt. Anybody who knew Mrs Flaherty knew that to criticize her cooking was sacrilege and the atmosphere downstairs was tense, to say the least.

'We're well out of it, Kiera my darlin', yes we are,' Bronagh said, tickling her under her chin. 'She just smiled at me, Moira,' she exclaimed delightedly.

'It's probably wind, Bronagh.' Moira was drawn to the window once more.

'What's got the ants in your pants anyway. Sure, it's only morning tea with the woman. You're not fine dining with the Queen of England.'

Bronagh was right, she was on edge, she couldn't help it. 'This is the first time we'll have been on our own for any length of time. I'm worried we won't have much to say to each other. Tom's family's very close and I know how eager he is for us to get to know one another.' Moira twisted her hands in her lap. 'The thing is, Bronagh, I'm so desperate for her to like me that I'm bound to make an eejit of myself.' The impression she'd had to date of Sylvia Daly was that of a pleasant, capable woman who didn't go in for flowery platitudes. She was the

A BABY AT O'MARA'S

sort of woman, Moira sensed, who'd be immune to the fecky brown-nosing so there was no point in even trying.

'Be yourself, Moira, and you'll have plenty to say to each other. You both love Tom and you're the mammy of her grandchild so don't be fretting about that,' Bronagh urged. Then, taking stock of her pale face grudgingly added, 'Go get yerself a custard cream. Sure, they've magic properties in them, so they do. It will settle you down but promise me you'll curb that tongue of yours. There's to be none of the swearing in front of Tom's mammy do you hear me?'

'I'll be as pure as the driven snow,' Moira said as she shot over to grab a biscuit before Bronagh revoked her offer. The phone rang just as her hand reached into the drawer.

'Moira you can answer that I'm busy with the babby.'

Moira sighed. The biscuit would have to wait and, picking up the phone, she put on the professional receptionist's voice she hadn't used since leaving her job on the front desk of Mason Price. 'Good morning, O'Mara's Guesthouse, you're speaking with Moira, how may I help?'

Bronagh looked suitably impressed.

'Oh, hello there, Moira. I wasn't expecting you to answer. I remembered you saying you lived over O'Mara's Guesthouse and I got the number out of the book.'

'I don't normally answer but I was on my way out the door and Bronagh our receptionist is holding Kiera.' Her voice trailed off realising she'd done a Mammy because even though she'd no idea who she was talking to, she'd filled them in on all her goings-on anyway.

'Sorry, you probably haven't a clue who you're talking to, have you?' The woman on the other end of the phone didn't wait for an answer. 'It's Lisa here. We met yesterday morning at the coffee morning. I was going to ask you for your telephone number but you left in a hurry and I didn't get a chance. I hope you don't mind me ringing you on your business line.'

Moira's eyes widened. 'Lisa, hi. No, you're grand. How're you doing?'

'I'm good, ta very much and I won't keep you but what I'm ringing you for is to see if you'd like to meet up for a walk on Friday. We could go for a coffee afterwards. I've rung Mona too and she's free so would you like to join us?'

Moira forgot all about her nervous tummy for a moment; she even forgot about the custard cream as her face broke into a wide grin. 'I'd like that, thanks, Lisa.'

Moira explained she wasn't driving at least not yet at any rate and given her proximity to St Stephen's Green it was decided they'd meet up there. A backup plan was made to go straight to a café Lisa knew off Grafton Street called Coffee and Cream if it was wet.

'Thanks, Lisa, I'll look forward to that.'

'Me too, and I'll be seeing you Friday then.'

Moira put the phone down and saw Bronagh watching her with a quizzical tilt to her head. 'Who was that then?'

'That was one of the girls I met at the coffee morning I went to yesterday. She was nice. We're meeting up on Friday with another girl, Mona. She was a good craic.' Moira felt inexplicably happy.

Bronagh smiled. 'Do you good that will.'

A young red-headed woman from Sligo emerged from the breakfast room at that moment pausing to chat before heading up to her room.

A BABY AT O'MARA'S

'It smells lovely in here,' she commented, her hazel eyes settling on the flowers that were delivered weekly.

'That will be this,' Bronagh said waving a can of air freshener. 'It's Arpège scented.' She didn't elaborate as to why she'd doused the area in the scent.

'That's lovely, that is.' She took the can and then asked Bronagh if she'd jot down the brand for her.

Moira shook her head. She couldn't stand the stuff; it made her feel Mammy was peeping over her shoulder each time she caught a whiff.

The young woman stood talking to them for a while longer telling them that she was in Dublin for a job interview and, she confided, she was desperate for it to go well as it was her dream position. Moira and Bronagh wished her the best of luck. She wasn't the only one feeling nervous that morning, Moira realised, taking Kiera from Bronagh and strapping her back in her seat.

Kiera's gaze never faltered as she watched her mammy with her plump little hands resting on either side of her face.

'Moira, I hope you've trimmed those nails of hers, she's after touching her face.'

'I can see that and I have, Bronagh,' Moira said, straightening up. This time when she peeked out the window she saw Sylvia's shiny blue Ford Focus pulling in alongside the kerb.

'She's here!' It was bang on ten o'clock.

'Would you like me to go outside and curtsey?' Bronagh asked, tongue in cheek, as the phone began to ring. 'G'wan with you. You'll be grand so long as you remember there's to be none of the language.'

Moira picked up the capsule and baby bag before opening the door and stepping out into a day that was somewhat gloomy. She hoped it wasn't an omen.

Chapter Nineteen

'Hello there, Sylvia,' Moira said opening the car's back door and manoeuvring the baby capsule in.

'Good morning, Moira, you're looking very well on it.' Sylvia Daly smiled, looking over her shoulder. 'And how's our princess today? Keeping you up at night, is she? I remember those days well!'

'She's grand, thanks, and she slept for four and a half hours straight last night which was a first.' The safety buckle clipped into place and Moira straightened, being careful not to slam the door as she closed it before sliding into the passenger seat.

'Thanks so much for picking us up, it's very kind of you.' Moira remembered her manners as she fastened her own seat belt. Sylvia, who'd just driven from Blanchardstown, where the Dalys still lived in the house where Tom had grown up, was nearly doubling back on where she'd come from by taking her and Kiera over to Castleknock. It would be a four-way trip for her. The sooner, Donal took her out for another lesson the better, she thought, giving the woman who, to all intents and purposes was her mammy-in-law a surreptitious once-over.

She was a very presentable woman, albeit practical with her hair cut stylishly short and her makeup limited to a lick of mascara and peachy coloured lipstick. She wore plain glasses behind which were eyes as blue as her son's that missed nothing. The fingers tapping the steering wheel lightly as they idled at the lights were adorned only by a plain gold band

and her nails were short ovals, buffed to a shine. Her perfume was crisp and fresh and didn't linger the way Mammy's did for hours after.

To Moira's surprise, she was also quite the chatterbox but then she shouldn't be surprised because Mammy had been present most of the times she'd been in Sylvia's company and nobody could get a word in when she got started!

Moira was happy to lean back in the seat and listen to the anecdotes Sylvia was sharing about Tom's childhood as the car purred its way over to the leafy suburb of Castleknock. As Sylvia pulled into a car park she lamented, 'He was always determined, Moira, so we knew when he said he wanted to be a doctor that that's what he'd be.'

Moira nodded, her hand reaching for the door handle as Sylvia stilled the engine. She could hear the pride in her voice. She wished she'd half of Tom's dedication. It was one of the many things she admired about him. She'd struggled to stick at much of anything which was why, she supposed, Mammy and Tom were determined she'd stick with college and get her fine arts degree.

It wasn't long before the two women were seated opposite one another in a light and bright café with the hum of conversation hovering on the air around them like the drone of bees.

'The owners are Danish,' Sylvia said, pulling her purse from her handbag.

That explained the clean, unfussy interior, Moira thought, looking about her.

Sylvia leaned forward conspiratorially to add, 'Their cinnamon rolls are to die for. Can I tempt you? My treat.'

A BABY AT O'MARA'S

'Oh, no, you don't have to, Sylvia. You came all that way to pick me up. I can get it.' Moira was half out of her seat.

Sylvia waved her back down. 'Moira, we're family. It's my treat,' she said firmly.

'Erm, well, that would be lovely thank you.' Moira watched as she made her way up to the counter. She was dressed fashionably but in a sedate manner, definitely a single strand of pearls sorta woman not the whole choker full, she thought, before turning her attention to Kiera who was smacking her rosebud lips. It was her way of letting her mammy know she was ready for her bottle. She'd best sort that out before she gave her lungs a workout, Moira decided, getting the bottle and formula dispenser out.

'They're just warming them for us,' Sylvia said, sitting back down and watching as Moira tipped the powder into the bottle.

'Would you like to feed her?' Moira asked as she shook it. She wasn't overly fond of others feeding Kiera. Tom was different of course and she was used to Mammy and Aisling. She shouldn't feel any different about Sylvia, she knew that but it served as a reminder that her daughter wasn't solely reliant on her for sustenance. Seeing Sylvia's face light up at the prospect reassured her she'd done the right thing.

'I'd love to, Moira. Would you like me to get her out of that?' She gestured to the capsule and Moira nodded.

'Yes, please.' She tested the milk, more out of habit than necessity because she knew it was tepid, before watching while Sylvia settled herself in the seat with Kiera in her arms.

'She's a precious wee dote, so she is,' Sylvia said, taking the bottle from Moira and holding it to Kiera's lips. 'Buon giorno,

Kiera. That's good morning in Italian,' she added for Moira's benefit.

The coffees and rolls arrived and Moira, seeing Kiera sucking contentedly on the bottle, tucked into hers with gusto making the most of having her hands free. Sipping her coffee, she debated telling Sylvia to sit Kiera up for a few seconds and give her a break from the bottle though she knew full well she'd had four—five babies, she corrected herself—remembering Aidan who'd passed away as a tot. As it happened, Sylvia instinctively sat Kiera up halfway through the contents of the bottle and winded her.

Tom was right she realised. Other people were perfectly capable of looking after their daughter.

Sylvia was right too, she thought, munching into the doughy treat. The roll was scrumptious.

'Good, isn't it?' Sylvia glanced across at her amused.

Moira nodded her mouth too full to speak.

When Kiera had drained the bottle, done another windy-pop as Sylvia called it and been settled back down in her capsule with the blanket tucked in around her, she took a sip of her coffee before breaking off a piece of the roll and popping it in her mouth.

'Thanks again, Sylvia,' Moira said. 'That was lovely.'

'You're welcome,' she mumbled. 'Tell me about your art, Moira. Tom says you're very good.'

It warmed her to know Tom spoke highly of her to his family and she found herself opening up to his mammy about what her art actually meant to her.

'I think it's a good thing, you know, you going back to college to finish your degree.'

A BABY AT O'MARA'S

Moira was pleased to hear this. She had wondered whether the decision to continue with her course was viewed as selfish. 'I wouldn't be able to if you and Mammy weren't helping us out, Sylvia. Thank you.'

'I'm looking forward to spending time with Kiera.' And glancing down at her, she whispered, 'Ah bless, look she's nodding off.'

Moira saw her lids were indeed fluttering shut, her hands balled into two fists just visible over the blanket tucked in around her. She gave the capsule a rock with her foot knowing that would send her off while Sylvia finished her coffee and cinnamon treat.

'I did enjoy that,' she said dabbing her mouth with the paper napkin. 'But I shall have to do a few extra sessions aqua jogging with the girls, I think. Do you go to any exercise classes, Moira?' She gave a small laugh. 'I should reword that, *did* you go to any exercise classes?'

'No. I do a bit of prannyummy breathing though. What's aqua jogging?'

Sylvia looked a little perplexed as to what prannyummy was but figured it was a new fandangled young person's exercise fad as she explained about wearing a flotation belt and how jogging in the water was a good form of exercise because it was gentle on your joints.

Moira was about to say, 'So it's jogging for old people,' when she remembered it wasn't her own mammy sitting opposite her.

'You're very welcome to come along and give it a go with me, Moira.'

Moira could think of nothing worse. The O'Mara girls didn't swim. Lounge on the beach in their swimwear, splash about in a pool or float on a lilo, yes but actual get your heart rate up and arms and legs a-going, no.

Poor Aisling had been the only sister to show potential at the inter-school swim sports but her career had been short lived on account of her showing her boobies to the row of fourteen-year-old boys who'd come along to see the girls lining up in their swimsuits only to get much more than they bargained for.

Aisling had dived in when the starting pistol fired and swum her teenage heart out to the finish line. She'd clambered out of the pool victoriously to collect her runner-up medal wondering why the cheers from the crowd were especially loud only to discover her swimsuit had come untied and was flapping about her waist. Mammy was mowing people down trying to get down the stand with a towel to cover her daughter and she gave the loudest of the lads a clip around his ear on her way past.

Just like *Jaws*, Aisling had refused to get back in the water after that hanging up her goggles and swim cap for the duration of her schooling. She'd a habit of doing things like that Moira thought, thinking of the Mo-pants-Tupperware-style evening at the church hall in Howth where she'd flashed a room full of pensioners. It must be something to do with her being the bustiest of the trio.

Anyways, suffice to say the O'Maras didn't swim per se and this was why she was at a loss to understand why the words, 'I'd like that, Sylvia,' trooped out of her mouth.

A BABY AT O'MARA'S

Sylvia sat back in her chair looking pleased while Moira did a few of the pelvic floors only it was all her insides doing the clenching because she had a feeling Sylvia was also the sorta woman who, if she said they'd do something, would be sure to put it into action.

To confirm this inkling, Sylvia said, 'Leave it with me then. I'll organise a time that works for you with Kiera.'

Moira smiled weakly. Maybe she could talk Andrea into coming along with her. It wouldn't be so bad if she were there too. She blinked, realising her mobile was ringing.

'Excuse me, Sylvia,' she said reaching down for it in the bag and answering it without thinking.

'Moira, it's me your mammy. I'm at the Tesco and I'm telephoning you. Sure, it's a marvellous thing this mobile.'

Moira regretted having answered although she was pleased Mammy was over her snit. 'That's nice, was there something you were wanting?'

'Can a Mammy not ring just to say hello to her daughter?'

'I'm busy at the moment, Mammy, I'll phone you later.'

'Where are you? I tried you at home but there was no answer so I'm ringing you mobile to mobile like.'

Jaysus what had she been thinking. Aisling was right, a monster had been unleashed. 'I'm at a coffee shop.'

'Who with? Are you after meeting up with one of those girls you got on well with at the mammy-baby coffee morning?'

'No, although I am meeting up with Lisa and Mona on Friday.'

'Ah, that's great altogether, Moira. So, who're you out and about with then?'

Moira decided there was only one thing for it, she tapped the phone, 'Mammy, I can't hear you. I think my battery's after going flat. I'll ring you when I get home.' She hung up and switched the phone off, shoving it back in the baby bag. She was only delaying the inevitable but at least when she spoke to Mammy later it would be out of Sylvia's earshot.

'Sorry about that,' Moira mumbled.

'It's not a bother. Now then, I suppose we should get on with the important matter of that little darling's christening,' Sylvia gave a besotted smile at Kiera before retrieving a hardback notebook from the handbag swinging off the side of the chair. The words Kiera's Christening were neatly written in the subject box.

She clearly meant business, Moira thought.

Chapter Twenty

'Honey I'm home,' Tom called out in his American sitcom voice closing the apartment door behind him as he barrelled into the living room.

Moira blinked. She must have fallen asleep and she hauled herself upright in time to tilt her chin up for a kiss. Tom's lips lingered on hers for a moment then he dumped his bag on the floor and raising an eyebrow asked, 'Coffee?'

'Yes, please, I can make it.' Moira made a half-hearted attempt to get up. She was groggy and must have slipped into a deep sleep. There were times like now when she felt worse for having had a nap but a coffee would sort her out, she thought. Poor Tom though was working at Quinn's tonight and the shot of caffeine was a necessity to keep him going.

He pushed her back down gently. 'Stay put. I can make it.'

'Thanks.' Moira watched him pad through to the kitchen, the sight of him making her smile as it always did. 'How was college?'

He looked back over his shoulder from the worktop. 'I nearly fell asleep listening to Professor Dumbledore droning on.'

Moira smiled at the Harry Potter reference but it faltered as she wondered what he was running on. His tank had to be close to empty what with his schedule of learning, study and work. She struggled to get through her day and she'd none of that going on. Mind you that would all change when she started back at college next week. The thought made her feel vaguely ill. 'Hopefully, Kiera's feeds will stretch out soon,' she said. 'Things will be easier then.'

Tom flashed her a rueful grin. 'I used to nod off in his lectures *before* we had Kiera. What about you then? How did it go with my mam?'

'She's a very organised woman,' Moira stated carefully. She knew how it worked. It was alright to bag one's own mammy or siblings when they were annoying but it was very much not okay for one's boyfriend or whatever Tom was these days to do so and vice versa.

'She is,' Tom concurred, oblivious to Moira's frown as he spooned instant coffee into the mugs he'd gotten out.

'She'd samples for me to choose from for the invitations and the catering sorted as well as the church...' Her voice trailed off as she realised he couldn't hear over the noise of the kettle and as she waited for it to finish boiling she thought back on how the warning signs had been there when Sylvia had clicked her pen down and opened the notebook all businesslike. She'd smoothed the page upon which there was already a list of names before angling it so as Moira could see.

'I've already jotted down who I feel should be invited on the Daly side of the family. I hope that's alright with you?'

It was strange this almost mammy-in-law business, Moira thought. They were tiptoeing around each other, both on their best behaviour. There was none of the riding roughshod over everything she was used to from Mammy.

'Of course, it is,' she said dipping her head and casting her eyes over the dozen or so names.

A BABY AT O'MARA'S

'Have you any idea how many will be coming on your side, dear?'

Moira retrieved the crumpled piece of paper on which she'd scribbled the names, Mammy had fired off at her the night before. She'd decided to run with Rosi's advice and despite her mixed feelings, she'd added her mysterious second cousin Sheridan and Great Aunt Dolly to the list.

Sylvia's eyes were like a wise owl's as they widened behind her glasses upon seeing the length of the list. 'My goodness, Moira, I didn't realise you came from such a large family.'

'Mmm, there's loads of us.' Moira shrugged apologetically wondering what Sylvia would make of her uncles or the Brothers Grimm as the sisters referred to them. She'd have to have a word with Mammy. They were her brothers therefore she could be in charge of ensuring they behaved themselves for once.

'Do you mind if I take this with me?' Sylvia asked gesturing to the paper. 'Only I thought I'd get the invitations printed off to save you a job. I know how busy you must be. I've brought some samples for you to take a look at so let me know which one you'd prefer.' True to her word, she produced an array of different card samples in varying shades of pink with embellished flowery fonts.

Moira wasn't a ditherer and she pointed to the middle one. 'That's lovely.'

Sylvia dimpled, 'I thought so too. Shall we run with that then?'

Moira nodded.

'I've a few thoughts on the catering too.'

Catering, what catering? Moira's palms suddenly felt clammy. She was thinking an afternoon tea of sausage roll type savouries, the heat and eat variety from Tesco along with some cakes and tea and coffee in the guests' lounge. There wasn't money for caterers on the tight budget she and Tom were existing on and certainly not for the number of people who were likely coming. She'd have thought Sylvia would have realised that. She didn't get a chance to put voice to any of this though as Sylvia carried on.

'I know a lady, she catered my friend's anniversary party, and everybody agreed the food was gorgeous and... she just happens to be available for Sunday the fifth of May.' Sylvia paused long enough to register Moira's blank expression.

She gave an exasperated sigh. 'Tom didn't tell you did he?'

'Tell me what?'

This time she rolled her eyes. 'Honestly, that son of mine, it goes in one ear and out the other. He was christened on the fifth of May. I thought it would be wonderful for Kiera's to be held on the same date, in the same church.'

'The same church?'

'Yes, St Mary's in Blanchardstown. It's where Jim and I were married and we had all our children christened there. Aidan's funeral Mass was held there too. I've checked and Father Simon's happy to hold the service then. I had the baptism committee tentatively pencil the date in. You don't need to do a thing other than provide me with a copy of Kiera's birth certificate and show up on the day! I know it's short notice but there's really nothing for you to organise.'

Moira felt a frisson of sadness for the Daly family's loss. She knew how Tom's brother, Aidan's death as a little fellow had affected all their lives. Perhaps it was fitting the christening should be held at their church. Still and all, she mused, it would have been nice to have been asked before any dates were decided on, tentative or not. And, it was awfully short notice given Patrick and Uncle Colin were travelling from Los Angeles for it. She didn't say this though, listening to Sylvia chatter on.

'Tom said you and your sisters weren't regular churchgoers and that your mammy attends church in Howth so I didn't think you'd mind if we held the service at our family church given our long history with it.'

Moira wasn't sure how she felt. She did need to grapple back some control though and in her brightest voice she chirped, 'Then, everybody could come back to O'Mara's for the after function.' This could be a good way of getting out of the paid catering Sylvia had in mind she thought to herself.

Sylvia toyed with the handle of her cup. 'Moira, it's rather a long drive from Blanchardstown to the guesthouse don't you think? And the parking's a nightmare. Sure, it'd be much easier to have it in the church hall. That way nobody needs to drive anywhere because they're already there.' She gave a tinkly laugh. 'Oh and, Moira, what I should mention is that Jim and I wanted Kiera's day to be on us. Our treat. She's our first grandchild after all.'

Moira blinked. She did want Kiera's christening to be special and the Moira of old would have snatched her hand off but the new mammy Moira found herself saying, 'It's a very generous offer Sylvia but really, there's no need. Tom and I will manage.' Even as she said it she hadn't clue as to how they would. There'd be no fancy invitations or catering for starters.

'Please, Moira, Jim and I want to. It would mean a lot to us both.'

How could she say no to that without causing offence? She'd thought and so she'd said, 'Well, it all sounds wonderful what you've got in mind, thank you, Sylvia and thank Jim for me too, won't you?'

'There's no need sure, we're family now.' Sylvia wrote a few things down in her notebook and then snapped it shut. 'Right then, Moira, now we've that all sorted what do you say we make the most of that little one having nodded off and pay a visit to the baby shop I mentioned to you on the phone last night? It's only round the corner and it has the most darling christening gowns.'

It dawned on Moira in that moment that mammy-in-laws weren't all that different from Mammies after all. Sylvia had just steamrolled over Kiera's christening by offering to bankroll it leaving her feeling as though she'd no option but to go along with her plans. Something else was bothering her too, but she couldn't pinpoint what it was.

Moira came back to the here and now. Was she being ungrateful? Because in a bag on their bed wrapped in tissue paper was an exquisite christening gown. It was white and covered in tiny stars with a tulle skirt. It even came with a bonnet which Moira had felt was a little over the top but Sylvia thought it and the dress were adorable and so she'd gone along with it. She was paying after all.

Despite the generosity of Sylvia and Jim, she was feeling perturbed. Sylvia had had her turn. She'd had five christenings for her own babies to plan whereas Moira had been on the outside looking in when it came to the arrangements for her baby's special day. She knew it wasn't intentional, Sylvia was caught up in the thrill of a new baby in the family and oblivious to how Moira felt. She wasn't a mind reader after all.

Tom plonked her coffee down in front of her as a mewling cry went up. 'Madam's awake,' he said.

This time Moira got up and told him to sit down. He was going to be on his feet for the best part of the evening anyway.

She returned with Kiera a nappy change later and put her in her daddy's arms while she sorted out her bottle. He'd flicked the television on to a cheesy gameshow. She knew he liked to stare mindlessly at the television for half an hour when he got in from college. He'd so much information buzzing about in that head of his, it was his way of deprogramming before he had to put his waiter smile on for the evening.

'Here we are, do you want to do the honours or shall I?' Moira asked holding the bottle out.

Tom reached out his hand for it. 'I will.'

The studio audience on the television cheered and clapped.

'I should go on Tell me the Facts, you know,' Tom said, arranging Kiera. 'I get the answers right more than most of the eejits who have a go. It'd be money for jam.'

Moira snuggled down next to him and stroked her daughter's downy head. 'If they had a Tell me the *fashion* Facts show or best mascara facts show I'd wipe the floor clean,' she said. Although she'd have to smarten up her act if she were to go on the tele she thought. She'd changed into her comfy tracksuit bottoms and a sweatshirt as soon as she'd got back in the door this afternoon. She wondered if Tom missed seeing her in her teeny-tiny red dress and the likes.

Her mind turned back to the christening. Her words would have to be chosen carefully because she didn't want Tom to think she sounded like an ingrate when she relayed the arrangements his mammy was keen to get underway and told him about the gown. Tact however had never been her strong point.

'Did you know your parents are insisting on paying for Kiera's christening?' Why did she have a snippy tone when she'd wanted to come across as conversational she wondered.

'Are they?'

'Yes, your mam was adamant.'

'Ah, well now, you don't argue with my mam,' Tom said.

Moira had got that impression alright. 'Tom, you didn't tell me your mammy wanted to have Kiera's christening on the fifth of May. It's only a couple of weeks away. It's very short notice for all those travelling for it.' Mind that could be a good thing; second cousin Sheridan and Great Aunt Dolly might not be able to make it. If lady luck was on her side the Brothers Grimm would be otherwise engaged too.

Tom looked up once he'd wiped the milk from Kiera's chin, sitting her up to wind her, at last detecting the annoyance in her voice. 'Sorry, Moira, I meant to tell you but it went out of my head.' He shot her an apologetic grin.

That grin of his usually worked wonders but now she'd started telling him about what had transpired with Sylvia she was beginning to feel thoroughly put out.

He studied her face for a moment. 'Is it going to be a problem?'

'No. It's just going to be a rush that's all.'

'Mam said not to worry, she'd help you sort everything.'

A BABY AT O'MARA'S

'Well, she's certainly done that, I don't have to do a thing. She's even bought Kiera's christening gown.'

'I know she can be a little pushy at times—'

A snorting sound escaped from Moira unbidden. 'You don't say.' She hadn't meant to say that either. This was all going pear-shaped and she could tell by the way Tom's face darkened she'd overstepped the mark. She'd broken the golden rule of bagging your partner's parent.

'She's only trying to help, Moira, and Kiera's her first grandchild. We're not in a position to lay anything much on, I'd have thought you'd have been pleased.'

'But, Tom, the service isn't even going to be at St Theresa's because you told her Ash and I don't go to church and Mammy attends over in Howth.'

'But that's true, isn't it?' He was bewildered. Women were an enigma, he thought, looking down at Kiera and wondering if she'd be a puzzle to him one day too.

'Yes but, Mammy's very fond of St Theresa's. She thinks Father Fitzpatrick's marvellous. He christened us all and married Ash and Quinn. And for your information, we do go. We go twice a year without fail at Easter and Christmas.' This was something Father Fitzpatrick was always quick to remark on when the O'Mara girls graced his inner sanctum with the sarcastic greeting of, 'I could set me calendar by you girls.'

Jaysus how was she going to tell Mammy, Moira thought. She'd not bear the news well.

'Ah,' Tom looked as though the penny had just dropped. 'You're worried as to how you're going to tell your mammy.'

Yes, she was, but it was more than that. There was something else bothering her but she couldn't figure out what it was.

'Moira, could you not just be grateful that you don't have to worry about it. You were after telling me it was all too much just the other day and now mam's taken the stress out of it for you, I'd have thought you'd have been pleased.'

He didn't get it because he was from Mars, all men were, Moira thought, her throat feeling tight with threatening tears. And that was another thing. She tipped so easily these days. She'd always been strong, not this blithering mess she seemed to have turned into. The last thing she'd wanted was to argue and so she did her best to soften her words as she asked. 'How am I going to tell my mammy that the reception's going to be held over in Blanchardstown and not here, at O'Mara's?'

Tom did have the grace to look a little sheepish at that and his voice had a conciliatory vibe to it as he replied, 'I don't envy you that Moira and I'm sorry Mam upset you. She wouldn't have meant to. She'd be beside herself if she knew she had. It's just Mam.'

Moira felt the last of the angry air hiss out of her. It wasn't his fault and she knew Sylvia thought she was helping. She was an ungrateful madam that was the problem.

The phone picked that moment to ring and Moira got up, padding over to it. She hesitated and looked over with a stricken face at Tom as a thought occurred to her. 'I bet you it's her.'

'Who?'

A BABY AT O'MARA'S

'Mammy. She's a sixth sense when I'm talking about her.' She nibbled her nail in between the demanding rings. 'I won't answer it.'

'Moira, you have to. It might be important.'

He was right, her hand reached out and she picked it up answering with a hesitant, 'Hello.'

'Moira? It's your mammy.'

Moira loved Tom she really did but right then she could have happily lobbed the phone right at him and told him to deal with Mammy. She would have too if he hadn't been holding Kiera.

Chapter Twenty-one

Nina sat alone at the table in the kitchen of the large Edwardian house she shared with six other flatmates she barely knew, and most of whom were either at work or still asleep in bed. The greasy smell of frying hung in the air as she nursed her coffee and stared at her last piece of toast. It had been a bonus to find the worktop was clear. The sink hadn't been piled high with dishes either.

The house was run a little like a hostel, with Francisco a fellow Spaniard who hailed from Granada and who was also the longest-running tenant, in charge. There was a roster pinned to the wall here in the kitchen listing who was down to do what chores, to ensure the house stayed reasonably clean, on what day.

Nina was always careful to tidy up after herself here in the kitchen and never to help herself to any of the named food in the fridge. She did her jobs on the weeks it was her turn and all in all was what her mother would have called a good girl, apart from the one time she'd not been, she thought ruefully. Her hands fluttered to her stomach and rested there briefly before she picked up the toast to nibble.

There was only Seamus, the Irish boyfriend of Sofie, a German girl, who was lax in ticking off his jobs. The atmosphere had been tense in the house whenever he, Sofie and Francisco were in the same room since Francisco had told him

A BABY AT O'MARA'S

if he wasn't going to pull his weight he and Sofie could move out.

Nina had seen Seamus with the vacuum cleaner in the living area the other morning and had assumed he'd decided it was easier to wield that than to join the mile-long queues of people waiting to view furnished flats in the city. Either that or Sofie had given him a talking to.

Nina sighed as she finished her breakfast, brushing crumbs from her lap and making her way to the sink. She'd eaten but she felt hollow inside. It was loneliness. She missed her friend Elena even though she knew if she were home she wouldn't see much of her. These days, Elena was living the life they'd talked about when they were teenagers. She was in Madrid working for a law firm. When she came home, Nina liked to listen to her stories of what life was like in the city. She wasn't envious though. She wouldn't change having had Ana for anything.

She missed Elena, she missed her parents, but most of all she missed Ana.

It had been hard for her to make friends here in Dublin mostly because she didn't go out like the others she house-shared with. There were only so many times you could say no before people stopped inviting you.

She liked Bronagh and the O'Mara sisters and got on particularly well with Moira but their chats had never been anything deeper than surface level. Moira was unaware of how she spent her time outside her working hours at O'Mara's, they all were. This was the way Nina liked it because she knew they'd feel sorry for her if they did know and she didn't want sympathy. She was here of her own choosing and the payoff, in the long run, would be worth it.

Her roommate Katica was the closest person to a friend she had here in Dublin and to be fair she hadn't stopped asking whether she'd like to come out with her. She'd always pause as she put her lip gloss on to ask if Nina would come and let her hair down. 'We will make some craic as the Irish say,' she'd grin at Nina. It made Nina laugh.

She liked Katica even if her half of the bedroom they shared was always a midden with clothes strewn everywhere. She'd a good heart and she'd confided in Nina once, not long after they'd begun sharing that she was glad to be away from Slovenia. She'd not had an easy childhood and she was hoping to stay here in Dublin. That had been the opener for Nina to tell her roommate her own story but the words wouldn't come and she'd stuck to what she told anyone who asked, that she was here to earn money to send home.

Sunday afternoon was the worst time of the week for her. She would sit in her room and write short stories to send home to Ana about things she'd seen in the week. Stories she hoped made her laugh. She'd always been good at writing and her mother had told her how much Ana loved receiving her funny anecdotes in the mail. She'd have written letters but she never had much in the way of news.

One particularly melancholic Sunday she'd decided to telephone Elena and not to think about what it would cost. Elena, being the friend that she was, had insisted she hang up and she'd called her back immediately. She'd poured her heart out that afternoon, crying down the phone as to how much she missed home and Ana.

Elena had told her that her parents had managed the restaurant all those years without an extension and that it

A BABY AT O'MARA'S

didn't matter if it had to wait a few years longer. What mattered was Ana. Nina had replied that she couldn't give her daughter much but that one day the restaurant would be hers. This was why she was here in this cold city. It was to ensure a future for her daughter. She'd had to forget her studies when she'd had Ana, she had no qualifications but one day, Abello's would be hers and she wanted her daughter to be proud of the part she'd played in ensuring it continued to open its doors for business. She was doing this for Ana.

Elena had talked about coming to Dublin to see her but Nina put her off. The sight of her friend here would only make her pine for home more.

She set about washing her breakfast things, recalling how she used to daydream as to what it would have been like if things had been different with Brando. She'd imagine a life in which they were a proper little family, him, her and Ana. All living above Abello's. The thing was though, what had attracted her to Brando in the first place other than his good looks was his free spirit. She hardly knew him. Not really, and she wasn't sure even if she did know how to contact him that she would have. How could she quash that free spirit? He'd talked of going further than Europe and she'd been dazzled by talk of pyramids in Mexico and abandoned cities in the mountains in South America. She wondered if he'd got there.

Brando wasn't aware of Ana's existence because by the time it had dawned on Nina she was pregnant all she had left to remember him by was his red bandana. She'd had no telephone number, no address, no clue as to anything about his life other than that he came from Rome and had no intention of settling down.

At her mother's insistence, she'd told Ana her father had passed away the first time she'd come home from playing at her friend, Gabrielle's house and asked where her father was.

'It's easier for the child that way,' her mother said but the lie didn't sit well with Nina. She knew given Ana's inquisitive nature she'd not be happy with such a simplistic answer as she got older. There would be questions about who his family were and why she'd never met them.

Nina picked up the tea towel and dried the bowl before placing it back in the cupboard. The thought of Ana's questions in the years to come made her head hurt. But her mother was right. How could she tell her daughter she knew nothing of her father other than he had been from Rome, handsome and charming, with a love of exploring new places? How he'd come along at a time when she'd been so restless as to the limits of the small world she inhabited that she'd got carried away and thrown caution to the wind.

Most of all though, how could she tell her she could never regret any of it because she had been given Ana as a result?

Would Ana forgive her for the fact she'd never know anything about her father?

Chapter Twenty-two

Toledo 1996

Brando meandered into the dining room just after eight on the evening he'd breezed into Nina's life. He paused to speak to her father who had just finished settling an early dining party's bill. Nina watched the exchange as she cleared the array of tapas dishes stacking them with practised ease. Her father was beaming and for some silly reason, she felt proud of Brando for winning him over like he had her with that easy smile of his.

Her father led him to a table set for two by the window and Nina admired the languid way in which Brando moved. He was like a panther and her father was like the chubby one from the silent films. Hardy or was it Laurel? The analogies made her smile.

A panther! She could imagine what Elena would say if she was to share this with her. She'd laugh and say she'd read far too many of the romance novels, Elena's mother was a fan of. It was true. She had.

Mrs De Leon had bookshelves full of well-thumbed paperbacks all featuring swooning heroines and swarthy males. Nina and Elena would giggle over them as they lay next to each other on Elena's bed flicking through for the racier chapters to read them out loud in breathy voices before fanning one another with the books in a fit of giggles.

Of course, neither girl would admit to actually enjoying the stories and they wouldn't be seen dead posing outside one of the umbrella cafés as they called them, a copy with a bare-chested, swashbuckling man with long hair and a moody look on his face in their hand. Oh no, when they were play-acting sophisticates in the shade of those umbrellas nursing a cold Coca-Cola for hours they'd each be holding a copy of *War and Peace* or *Anna Karenina!*

Nina carried the dishes through to the kitchen where her mother's hands were doing a million different things as she ladled, salted and tore off the orders from the wire above the oven. She put the dishes down on the bench and then, licking her lips, picked up the steaming meal for the middle-aged man eating alone and strode back out to the restaurant. She placed it in front of him with a flourish and then out the corner of her eye she saw a man wave out to her from where he and his wife were sitting in the far corner. She ignored him and made straight for the table her father had placed Brando at.

The window, with the dark street outside, was like a frame around him she thought approaching.

He was studying the menu and he looked up when she greeted him. His eyes crinkled at the corner as he smiled up at her warmly. She could smell his shampoo she realised inhaling the fresh faintly coconut scent of his damp hair hoping she didn't look silly as she grinned back at him.

'Nina!' He said this as though surprised they should have met up again.

She tried to retain a degree of composure as she asked, 'Is your room comfortable?'

'Si, very. It feels bello, erm, bueno?'

A BABY AT O'MARA'S

Nina nodded her head affirming he had the Spanish word for good.

'...to put clean clothes on.'

Her gaze swept over his T-shirt noting he was a fan of Hootie & the Blowfish. She liked the band too and looked forward to the day she and Elena could go to concerts and see and hear something other than the traditional music served up here. She was fed up with castanets and longed for a heavier, modern beat.

'So then,' Brando gestured to the menu what would you recommend a poor, malnourished traveller have for his dinner?'

The way his cheek dimpled each time he smiled at her was doing funny things to her heart rate and she was unsure how her legs would carry her through to the kitchen to peg his order to the wire. She took a steadying breath and tried to pretend he was the fat man sitting a few tables in front of Brando slurping his gazpacho down.

'That's easy,' she said. 'You must try my mother's cocida madrileño. It's normally served in winter but given it is the best in all of Spain and people travel from far and wide to taste it, she serves it all year round.'

'Then that is what I will have.' He snapped the menu shut and Nina took it from him turning away lest her face give away the thoughts racing through her head.

How she managed not to make a show of herself throughout the evening as she took orders, carried steaming dishes and cleared dirty tables, Nina didn't know. Each time she risked a glance over to where Brando was seated he would catch her eye and she'd feel as though they were exchanging secrets.

He eked out his meal which he declared to be the best he'd ever eaten and insisted Nina pass this on to her mother. He polished off a dessert and then sat on a beer while the last of the tables slowly cleared out.

Finally, Nina turned the sign in the door to closed and as her father was in the kitchen helping her mother she decided to accept Brando's offer for the second time that day to sit with him while he drank his beer.

Her feet ached as she slid into the chair opposite him and before she had a chance to worry over what she would say to him he had her laughing with his impersonation of the fat man and his gazpacho.

Their conversation was easy as he lit a cigarette and spoke about his family. She sat watching the smoke curl upwards as he told her he was the oldest son, one of four, and how his mamma always wailed at him to come home when he telephoned. His papa would snatch the phone from her and tell him he was wasting his life bumming around Europe and what did he think he was playing at? He said it only made him all the more determined to keep going.

Nina envied him as she watched him draw down the nicotine. She was a good daughter and she kowtowed to the guilt card every time. As if to prove this point she shot out of her seat as though she'd been scalded when her father cleared his throat in the doorway of the kitchen. He gave her a hard stare and told her she was needed in the kitchen.

A BABY AT O'MARA'S

Brando ground out his cigarette and apologised to her father for taking up Nina's time. He got to his feet pushing the chair in and then stretched.

'I was telling her the meal was buonissimo,' he kissed his fingers and Nina wondered what his lips would feel like on hers. 'Now, if you'll excuse me, it's been a long day.'

Her father nodded, his expression having softened at this praise of his wife's cooking and her mother puffed up with pleasure as he repeated the compliment to her on his way through to his room. He hesitated long enough to meet Nina's eyes as she appeared in the kitchen weighed down by the dirty dishes she'd quickly gathered up so as to give her father no cause for complaint. She held her breath hoping he would not breathe a word of their plans to meet up after Mass the following day so she could act as tour guide because she knew her parents wouldn't allow it.

He opened his mouth then closed it thinking better of whatever it was he was going to say before wishing them all goodnight.

~~~

THE MASS HAD GONE ON forever, the priest's monotone voice echoing around the vast chamber of the cathedral the tourists flocked to see but at last, Nina stepped outside the darkened interior and into the mid-morning sunshine. It was blinding and they all stood blinking for a moment. She was flanked either side by her parents and behind her, the ancient stone walls of the gothic Catedral de Toledo glowed white.

Elena she saw when her eyes had adjusted was already outside. She too was dressed in her Sunday best as she stood with her back to her, fidgeting alongside her parents who were in conversation with the Rodriguezes. They'd brought their new baby along to the Mass and Elena's mother was peering into the shawl she was wrapped in.

'Mama, I'm going to Elena's.'

'Nina, your mama needs your help in the kitchen,' her father said but his wife nudged him. 'Let her go, she'll only be young once.'

Nina looked hopefully at her father who waved her away with her hand. She flashed a grateful smile at her mother, trying to imagine her when she was young. She couldn't envision a time when she hadn't been married to her papa and her hands hadn't smelled of onions and garlic.

Her father's voice trailed after her as he told her to be home mid-afternoon at the latest but Nina let the words fall on deaf ears. She was free!

She sneaked up behind Elena and placed both hands on her friend's shoulders causing her to jump and giggle. They linked arms, whispering over the ridiculously tight skirt Senorita Morales who fancied herself a film star was wearing. They giggled all the harder seeing Senora Perez jab her husband with her elbow when his eyes lingered on the senorita's undulating backside as she made her way down the cobbled street.

Elena's father shot them a disapproving look and Nina dragged her friend away out of earshot. She was fit to burst with the news that she would soon be showing a handsome Italian backpacker the hidden delights of Toledo.

Elena's eyes were gratifyingly round upon hearing this.

A BABY AT O'MARA'S

Nina saw her father out the corner of her eye waving out to her. She looked across the dispersing crowd to see him tap his watch to remind her not to be late back.'

'Si, Papa,' she called out as he nodded and set off with her mother for home. She and Elena skipped off in the opposite direction.

Nina had arranged to meet Brando outside Catalina from school's family's chocolate shop. They laughed, picturing Catalina's round face if she were to catch sight of Nina and the handsome Italian. It would be all over school come Monday for sure, they agreed.

'I am so jealous. I have to go home and help my mama cook lunch while you gad about the town with a sexy Italian.' Elena grinned and, telling her friend not to do anything she wouldn't do which they both knew wasn't very much at all, she hugged her goodbye.

The butterfly wings began to beat in her tummy as she watched Elena go and she hoped she wouldn't have to wait long because she was beginning to feel so nervous she might forget her offer to be tour guide and run home. She could feign nonchalance when she saw him next and say their meeting slipped her mind.

Then she saw him and she knew as she watched his lean, long-limbed stride cut a path through the busy square that she wouldn't go anywhere.

Chapter Twenty-three

Moira's ears were still burning from the ticking off she'd had from her mammy the night before as she packed the baby bag the following morning. The conversation played out in her mind for the umpteenth time.

Mammy had been asking if she'd managed to get the battery on her phone sorted and Moira had bitten her lip knowing she'd have to mention the christening. She'd need to give those who were travelling to be there warning it was now only three weeks away come Sunday, especially Patrick and Uncle Colin who were planning on flying in from Los Angeles.

Cindy, Patrick had informed Mammy during their last chat, was on the fence as to whether she could make Kiera's big day because her role as a television, feminine products ambassador was keeping her very busy of late. She was fond of telling them whenever Patrick put her on the phone, that in Hollywood you were only ever as good as your last advert. That made her a very good tampon spokeswoman, Aisling had sniggered to Moira the last time she'd spoken to the woman destined to be her sister-in-law.

So, with trepidation, Moira had taken a deep breath and come clean with the news of the short timeframe that had now been decided upon due to the connection with Tom's christening. This in itself had not gone down well with lots of spluttering and carry on about how could she expect people

A BABY AT O'MARA'S

to come at such short notice? Despite this, Moira felt Mammy would have come to terms with the change of date.

The fact that the christening dress had been bought, however, with Sylvia Daly being the one to zip-zap the credit card, had been greeted not with spluttering but something far worse, a sniffy silence that oozed hurt.

In for a penny, in for a pound or however the saying went, Moira thought, sounding the death knell. The service and afters would not be held at St Theresa's and O'Mara's, she announced, but rather the whole shebang would be at St Mary's in Blanchardstown, the Daly family's church.

Mount Mammy had erupted.

Moira had held the phone away from her ear scowling over at Tom who was, she was sure, deliberately not looking at her as he fussed over Kiera. By the time her mammy had moved on to how would the O'Mara family ever be able to show their faces in St Theresa's again and what would poor Father Fitzpatrick make of such a snub? Moira had had enough. She was tired and she couldn't be dealing with this.

'It is what it is, Mammy, and if you don't like it then don't come!'

She hadn't hung around to hear what Mammy would have to say to that as she disconnected the call. She'd left the phone off the hook and turned her mobile off. Tom didn't say a word which was a good thing because the way Moira was feeling she was certain had he offered anything up they'd have fallen out. Especially as he'd be off to Quinn's shortly leaving her to deal with the fall-out if her mammy was to ring back.

She'd put the kettle on to make a cup of tea then and as she'd wrenched the fridge open her eyes had alighted on the bottle of unopened white wine nestling alongside the milk. She stared at the green frosted glass and for a moment she could taste the chilled tang of that first sip of wine where the grape was sharp and the flavour set your mouth aquiver. She was salivating with longing.

She'd imagined the glugging sound as she poured the wine into a glass and the knot in her shoulders loosening with each sip as her racing thoughts slowed.

The sound of Kiera's cry had brought her back from the brink and she'd retrieved the milk closing the fridge firmly.

It had frightened her that moment and when she'd lain in bed later, instead of dropping off to sleep as soon as her head hit the pillow as she'd done since Kiera's birth, her mind wandered back to the not so long ago days when she'd liked a drink a little too much.

She wasn't an alcoholic though. An alcoholic was someone you'd see pushing a shopping trolley with all their worldly belongings piled high in it. An alcoholic sat on the Ha'penny Bridge with their hand out or propped up the bars of the hardened drinkers' pubs of Dublin.

She knew these were clichés and even if she wasn't an alcoholic per se, she knew her drinking hadn't been doing her any favours. She'd been a timebomb waiting to get herself into an even bigger mess than the one she'd nearly gotten into with a married man no less.

She thought back now on that time with Michael with disbelief. It was like she'd been a different person back then.

Lying in bed listening to the sounds of the guesthouse with one ear half-cocked for Tom coming in from Quinn's she reminded herself of all the times she'd woken up with a banging head. Her head would only get worse as the nausea would set in which was partly the booze and partly brought about by the flashbacks of what she'd gotten up to the night before.

When she got down to the nitty-gritty of it all, Moira didn't much like herself when she drank. She made better choices and was happier in herself when she didn't. It was simple, and once she'd made her mind up that enough was enough she'd never looked back.

Having a baby though, well, it was hard. So much harder than she'd thought it would be. She'd known there would be sleepless nights and a never-ending rota of routine and that was okay because she could handle that. She was a girl who was used to burning the candle at both ends. What she was struggling with was the self-doubt that was eating away at her as to whether she was a good mammy. Had Kiera drawn the short straw being allocated Moira O'Mara as her mammy?

She'd tossed the covers aside then, padding across the room to look down at Kiera who was in a deep sleep. She placed her hand gently on her chest wanting to feel the rise and fall of it because sometimes her daughter slept so deeply it was frightening.

Moira breathed out herself feeling the steady rhythm of Kiera's breathing. She knew then and there that she wouldn't open that wine and take a sip no matter how tough the going got. She might feel she was letting her daughter down with not having been able to breastfeed and second-guessing everything she did where she was concerned but one thing she did have control over was her ability not to get back on the sauce because she refused to be the sorta mammy who put herself first.

It was a revelation that the world which had once firmly revolved around herself now orbited around her daughter.

Today however was a new day. The sun was shining and had washed away her dark thoughts from the night before. Donal, good man that he was—why Moira repeated that phrase to herself whenever she thought of him since the driving lesson she didn't know— would have talked sense into her Mammy. She'd have had the chance to sleep on the arrangements and come to terms with them too.

As Moira chucked the empty packet of baby wipes aside and cast about for a packet to put in the baby bag she was even hopeful that she might accept them all with good grace. 'No way, it's Mammy yer talking about,' she said receiving a sweet smile from Kiera. 'Perhaps we could suggest she be in charge of your holy communion when the time comes, Kiera, that might appease your nana.' Desperate times called for desperate measures.

She'd half expected a phone call from her this morning and had found the silence of the telephone Tom must have put back on the hook when he came in last night unnerving.

Everything had seemed quieter that morning in the apartment. Aisling was buzzing about in the guesthouse somewhere or other, Quinn was still in bed and Tom had gone to college kissing her on her forehead and telling her to have a good day as she lay in bed waiting for Kiera to wake up. Even she'd seemed quieter that morning as she sucked on her hand in her cot, instead of her usual lusty wake-up cry.

She'd rather Mammy had rung so they could clear the air and get on with things. Her baby girl was being christened after all. It was supposed to be a joyous occasion to mark and press

A BABY AT O'MARA'S

into a family photo album. Not the nightmare it was turning into.

She could have telephoned Mammy and put herself out of her misery, she mused retrieving a half-used packet of wipes and going through the bag a final time, zipping it up and satisfied she was prepared for any calamity that morning. She knew however that trying to jolly up a sulking Mammy was akin to prodding a bear with a sore tooth. Not a good move. She was best left to it.

With a sigh, Moira picked her daughter up making sure the pom-pom hat, Bronagh's mammy had kindly knitted her covered her ears and then, hefting the bag up onto her shoulder, she cast one last look at the telephone. It remained silent.

Chapter Twenty-four

Moira called out the brightest good morning she could manage as she made her way carefully down the stairs arriving on the second-floor landing. The fellow whom she'd greeted was in the process of unlocking the door to Room 8 and he didn't so much as glance over his shoulder.

Moira pulled a face at his retreating back as he closed the door with a resounding click whispering to Kiera, 'Manners don't cost a thing.' She hesitated, thinking about what she'd just said. 'Ah Jaysus, Kiera pretend I didn't just say that. Sure, it's the sorta thing your nana would say.' She shook her head and continued down the stairs.

There was no sign of Ita on the first-floor landing and no sound of a humming hoover either. That girl, Moira thought, frowning and pausing momentarily as she debated going to find her. No, she'd no time for that she decided and besides, it was up to Aisling to sort her out.

The pram was kept folded up in a storage cupboard beside the stairs leading down to the basement and Mrs Flaherty's eagle ears must have heard the creak of the cupboard door opening because Moira heard her thundering up the stairs as she hauled the pram out with one hand. The cook appeared beside her red-faced and smelling of bacon fat with her plump arms reaching out for Kiera.

A BABY AT O'MARA'S

'Here we are, here's Mrs Flaherty come to see you Kiera my lovely. Let me hold her for you while you sort that pram, Moira.' It was an order, not an offer.

She seemed in good form this morning, Moira thought, noting her beaming smile and rosy apple-red cheeks as she passed her daughter to her. There can't have been any Foxy Loxy visits the night before or guests who'd dared complain an egg wasn't done to their liking.

She half listened, fiddling with the pram, as the cook told her and Kiera about the Canadian couple who'd said her full Irish had been the best breakfast in all of Ireland. Moira knew as soon as Kiera was old enough she'd be feeding her up on the sly with crispy bacon rashers and the like just as she had her Patrick, Roisin and Aisling when they were younger. Mrs Flaherty was one of life's feeders and her greatest pleasure in life was seeing someone enjoy her food.

Bronagh's dark head popped around the corner just then to see what was going on and Aisling appeared at the bottom of the stairs muttering on about Ita and that fecking phone of hers she was so fond of.

Moira, who could feel her blood pressuring rising on account of not being able to get the pram to click into place, grumbled, 'It's busier than Grand fecking station in here.'

'Grand *Central* station,' Aisling corrected her.

'Feck off, Aisling,' Moira rebutted, wondering why it was Tom could get this fecking overpriced Rubik's cube on wheels disguised as a pram to lock into place first time, every time. She'd never been any good at puzzles, she sighed, trying once more to no avail and feeling her foot twitch with the urge to kick it.

'I can take Kiera for you now Mrs Flaherty,' Bronagh bossed, stepping forward. 'I'm sure you've a full house needs seeing to downstairs.'

Moira and Aisling held their breath because for a moment it looked as if Mrs Flaherty would repeat Moira's sentiment to her sister seconds earlier. For a woman who bore a strong resemblance to Old Mother Hubbard in the children's nursery rhyme, she'd a mouth on her like a navvy when her blood pressure began to rise and it was clearly rising now.

'Everybody's perfectly happy and enjoying their breakfast thanks very much, Bronagh, but I think I can hear that fax going like the clappers out there, best you go tend to that,' Mrs Flaherty sniped through gritted teeth, holding Kiera closer to her ample bosom as she took a step back from the eager receptionist.

Bronagh and Mrs Flaherty eyed one another as though they were about to duel it out at the O.K. Corral.

'Bronagh,' Aisling said, stepping in, 'Did you send confirmation of their booking to the Australian tour party? Only I promised we'd get back to them this morning.'

Bronagh swung around huffily and marched back to reception.

'Here let me do it,' Aisling said, seeing Moira getting redder in the face as she continued to tackle the pram.

Moira stepped back, hands raised in surrender. 'How did you do that?' she demanded a nanosecond later hearing a loud click to signify the pram was now fit for purpose as Aisling did something with her boot and the metal bar near the basket beneath it.

A BABY AT O'MARA'S

'It's easy, all you do is kick that down and voila! You're good to go.'

Moira shook her dark hair. 'Feck off with your voilas. I tried that and nothing happened.' She was beginning to wish she'd stuck with her original choice of a simple three-wheeler buggy.

She cast her mind back to the day when, with her belly like a beach ball, she'd been stood in the Mothercare shop with Tom staring at one such store model. She'd disappeared into a fantasy whereby she'd been clad in sleek black running gear, a sweatband thingamabob holding her hair back from her face. She was a majestic gazelle pounding the pavements of Dublin city as she multitasked by jogging and giving her baby fresh air with one-handed ease.

As Mammy always said, she'd a tendency to take things to the extreme and so it was in this fantasy people were stepping out of the way of this jogging apparition and elbowing each other to say, 'Sure she deserves a medal. Fair play to her. Having a baby hasn't slowed her down at all. She's running like the wind. Look at her go.'

'Moira,' Tom had nudged her. 'Why are you jogging on the spot?' His beloved wasn't the lightest at present and it was like a baby elephant was jiggling about in the middle of Mothercare.

She'd blinked and told Tom she needed to ask Rosi's advice as to what sorta pram they should go with. She'd dug her phone out and hit speed dial for her sister uncaring of the call charges given the importance of the matter at hand.

Roisin, pleased to be consulted and hearing of Moira's jogging fantasy, had told her sister the Moira she knew had never liked getting hot and sweaty unless it was in a Swedish sauna. Or, doing the riding and having a baby wasn't going to change that. The clincher for the pram they'd ended up purchasing, that would have been at home in the days of perambulators and parasols, was Roisin telling her how lovely it was to walk through the park talking face to face with your babby. You couldn't do that with a buggy, she'd said.

'You've got to have the magic touch is all,' Aisling said, unperturbed by her sister's language. 'Where are you off to anyway?'

'I'm meeting some mammies over in the Green, we're feeding the ducks and then going for coffee.'

Aisling smiled at her sister, pleased she'd made some new friends with whom she could compare mothering notes.

'I've some bread I was going to toss over the wall into the gardens you can take with yer,' Mrs Flaherty said as Bronagh appeared around the corner once more.

'I'll hold the baby Kiera for you while you get the bread for the ducks, Mrs Flaherty.'

'No, no, you're grand, Bronagh, sure Moira's got two legs, she can run down and get it. The exercise will do her good.'

Moira didn't know what that was supposed to mean and with a sigh, she disappeared downstairs for the bread. Reappearing a minute later she wasn't sure what had transpired in that short burst of time but Bronagh was now holding Kiera and Mrs Flaherty was rubbing her arm as though it were paining her.

'You might as well know,' Moira said, deciding not to ask as she shoved the bread into the pram's basket. 'That the christening is being held three weeks on Sunday at St Mary's

A BABY AT O'MARA'S

over there in Blanchardstown. It's the Dalys' family church. We're having afters there too. You'll get a formal invitation as soon as they've been printed.'

Three sets of eyes widened and Moira squirmed under their gazes as she straightened up.

'Does Mammy know?' Aisling demanded.

'Yes, what did Maureen say?' Bronagh asked.

Mrs Flaherty forgot about her sore arm and had begun crossing herself.

'She wasn't happy,' Moira said, refusing to look any of them in the eye.

'But why the Dalys' church?' Aisling asked.

'Why not?' Moira snapped, 'It's not all about the O'Mara's you know. The Dalys are just as much a part of Kiera's life. Why shouldn't it be held at their church?'

Aisling held her hands up in defence. 'Fair play but why couldn't you have compromised and had the morning tea here afterwards like we all assumed you would? You know it would mean a lot to Mammy.'

Bronagh and Mrs Flaherty were nodding their agreement and Moira was feeling very much on the back foot as her head began to throb and her face heated up.

'Mrs Daly, I mean Sylvia, pointed out it was a long way for guests to travel after the service and that it made more sense to have it in the church hall. She's organising the catering.' Moira decided to withhold the information that she was paying for the catering.

'Well, I don't blame Mammy for being upset.' Aisling sniffed and for the third time that morning, Moira told her big sister to feck off.

This time Aisling bit back. 'I don't know what's got into you, Moira, you're not normally such a fecky brown-noser.'

Moira made a noise that was half snort and half cough of indignation. 'Me, a fecky brown-noser? You're the one who's too bloody scared to tell her upstairs she's a lazy mare in case you upset Mammy's friend.'

'This isn't about me, Moira.'

Moira pulled a face at her sister. The thing was she knew Aisling was right. She'd not wanted to put Tom's mammy's nose out of joint and so she'd not spoken up about what she wanted but in doing so she'd gone and dislocated her own mammy's nose so to speak. She didn't like being in the wrong. Something else wasn't sitting right with her either but whatever it was refused to formulate itself into a coherent thought.

'Bronagh, I've got to go,' she blustered wanting to put distance between the trio of women who clearly thought she should have come to a compromise with Sylvia. She wheeled the pram toward her.

Bronagh, deciding now wasn't the time to put her penny's worth into the conversation, settled Kiera into the pram as Mrs Flaherty responded to a bell ringing downstairs.

She felt Aisling's eyes on her and she swung around. 'If it were up to me I'd cancel the whole fecking thing.' It was true. She wanted to forget about it. Why couldn't she and Tom just have a private christening ceremony for the three of them and go and have a pub lunch afterwards? What a weight off her shoulders it would be to forget about what everybody else thought they should do!

She didn't wait to hear what Aisling had to say as she wheeled the pram past her.

A BABY AT O'MARA'S

Bronagh trotted as fast as her pencil skirt would allow her to the door and she held it open. As Moira mumbled thanks and made to pass, she rested her hand on Moira's forearm for a moment.

The act of solidarity saw a tear roll down Moira's cheek.

'Now listen to me, Moira O'Mara. Don't you be worrying your head about it all. Sure, it's *one* day. Your mammy will get over it and Aisling's only got her knickers in a knot because she's fed up to the back teeth with Ita. What matters is that wee dote right there.'

Moira flashed a watery smile, 'You're right. Thanks, Bronagh.'

'Not at all, now go and enjoy yourself with your mammy friends and forget all about it.' Moira pushed the pram out into the spring sunshine.

Chapter Twenty-five

The bright blue sky, punctured with cottonwool ball clouds, lifted Moira's spirits as she pushed the pram under Fusiliers' Arch into the Green. The days of dashing across the busy road outside the guesthouse were long gone now she had precious cargo in tow. So were the days of tottering about in impractical footwear.

The temperature was positively balmy by Dublin standards she thought, feeling the tension leave her because it was impossible to frown on such a beautiful day. She followed the path decorated with daffodils deeper into the Green pausing to point out to Kiera the plump pink flowers dripping from a cherry blossom tree overhead. So engrossed was she in tracking a bee's flight path with her finger that she never heard the excited chatter of the Japanese tourists.

The party was being marched through the park by a tour guide who was jabbing the sky with an umbrella as she led the way. Cameras whirred and clicked in her and Kiera's direction but Moira was oblivious.

Two matronly Irish women laden with Dunnes Stores bags paused to see what all the hoo-ha was about. 'Sure look, it's your Demi Moore wan. She's been popping out the little Bruce Willis babies left right and centre so she has. That one there's probably called FooFiFum or FooFoo Pie or the like. I was reading all about it in a magazine at Mary's salon just the other day when I had my perm done. What is it with the Hollywood

A BABY AT O'MARA'S

people calling their children strange names? What's wrong with a good old-fashioned name like Derbhilla or Niamh?' Mrs Dooley said to her sister, Fidelma.

'Sure you know yourself those magazines are years out of date, Grainne. Mary's still got her communion money so she has.'

''Tis true enough. She wouldn't spend Christmas that wan.' They both lapsed into silence lamenting the meanness of their local hairdresser.

The sisters were on a shopping trip in the big smoke and had travelled from the small village of Ballyspur overlooking the sea.

'Do you think we might be asked to give a talk at the next Probus meeting about having seen a Hollywood star in the flesh like?' Fidelma asked.

Grainne hadn't thought of that and it put the spring back in her step. 'I'm certain of it, Fidelma.' The two women carried on their way.

The tulips were a carpet of red in their flowerbeds and Moira, unaware of the conversation that had just played out, admired them as she made her way to the duck pond. She trundled over the stone bridge and spied Lisa and Mona already spread out on a picnic rug. Two prams, every inch a perambulator like Moira's, were parked up alongside them. She waved over and reaching them nudged the brake down on the pram. 'How's the craic?'

Lisa shaded her eyes and grinned up at Moira. 'Me and Eva are grand but Mona's not had a good night.'

'Don't get me started.' Mona shook her head.

Her hair looked like fire in the sunshine, Moira thought. Tallulah was cradled in Mona's arms being fed by her mammy.

'I'm lucky if I've had three hours sleep. Tallulah's going to have to be surgically removed from these when the time comes.' Mona dipped her head toward her breasts. 'The nurse is after telling me it's a comfort thing and she's not going to be Ireland's biggest baby so I suppose that's something.'

Moira laughed.

'I read a letter in one of those parenting mags, you know the ones where there's a prize for the top letter?' Lisa said.

The other two women nodded. 'It said being a mammy to a newborn is thirty-three per cent nursing a baby that needs to burp, thirty-three per cent burping someone who wants to nurse and thirty-four per cent poo.'

Moira laughed.

'That's my life alright,' Mona lamented but she was grinning.

'We've a glorious day for it,' Lisa said, watching as Moira fished the quilt out of her baby bag.

'We have,' Moira agreed, flapping out Mammy's handiwork. She spread it next to where Eva who was lying on her purple blanket enjoying being outside was kicking her legs. 'Hello, Eva.' Two eyes blinked up at her.

'They've gone darker than when I met you at Cliona's.'

Lisa nodded. 'They're changing alright, she's going to have my brown eyes. Her dad's are hazel.'

Moira eyed the quilt and launched into the story behind it as she plucked Kiera from the pram and laid her down on it. They both laughed. Lisa reached over and took Kiera's tiny hand. 'She looks so sweet in those knits.'

A BABY AT O'MARA'S

'We've been inundated with cardigans, booties and hats,' Moira replied, feeling a burst of maternal pride as she looked at her daughter who was smiling at nothing in particular.

'Uh-oh, somebody's busy,' Lisa said seeing her daughter's face flush red. She fetched her changing mat, a clean nappy and wipes from the bag beneath her pram and came back to kneel in front of Eva. 'My husband, Matt, keeps blaming his farts on poor Eva here,' Lisa said as she set about changing her. 'The dog's had a reprieve since she came along.'

Their burst of laughter turned a few heads and the laughs continued as they began chatting about the stupid comments people made when you had a newborn.

'My sister's always after telling me Kiera's awake when she's howling blue murder. As if I didn't know,' Moira said.

Lisa and Mona nodded.

'My mam does that,' Mona said. 'She thinks she's being helpful.'

'Do you know the only decent piece of advice on being a mammy I've been given came from my auld nan,' Lisa said thoughtfully. 'She told me to always trust my instincts where Eva's concerned.' Lisa tapped the side of her nose and said, 'My nan said a mammy always knows when something's not right with her baby. The rest of it has been things like let her cry a bit and then she'll sleep or, sleep when she sleeps. I mean like there's nothing else that needs doing in the house and my personal favourite, put her down drowsy but awake. I can tell you right now it didn't work.'

'Don't forget the brown sugar in the juice for the constipation,' Moira piped up.

'Ah Jaysus, I forgot about that one.'

'People can be very annoying.' Mona added. 'I'm constantly asked, are you sure she's really hungry again? Erm, yes I fecking well am.'

'I hate it when people ask me if she's a good baby,' Lisa said wiping Eva's bottom with a practised hand. 'All babies, are good babies.'

'Do you know what I'd reply? I'd say, yes although I've had to ask her to stop robbing banks.' Mona's grin was wicked.

'That's a good one. I'll remember that,' Lisa replied, taking a mental note.

'I used to be good at the fast comebacks,' Moira said, her gaze turning to the duck pond as she watched another mother with a toddler running rings around her frantically trying to stop him from falling in.

'Your brain goes to mush, doesn't it? It's the broken sleep,' Lisa said.

Moira nodded, looking past the now captured tot to where the sunlight was dancing on the water. In the background, was the rippling sound of the waterfall that had seemed enormous when she was a child. 'I don't know how I'm going to cope with college next week, to be honest.'

'You'll cope. You'll look back in a year's time and wonder how you did it but you'll cope,' Mona said.

'I feel guilty about leaving her.' She pulled the hat up where it had slipped down over one of Kiera's eyes.

'That's a mammy's lot, I'm afraid but it's not as if you're leaving her with strangers. She'll be grand. It's you who'll be doing the worrying,' Lisa said, sticking the tabs down on the nappy.

A BABY AT O'MARA'S

'I know, you're right.' A swan and her entourage glided past. 'They're beautiful, aren't they? Animals know instinctively what to do when it comes to their offspring. I wonder why we don't,' Moira stated, watching the peaceful scene.

'That's the thing though, Moira. I think we do but then the helpful, not helpful advice starts and we wonder if we *were* right in the first place,' Lisa said, pulling Eva's tights back up. 'Or I am I the only one who constantly questions herself?'

'No, not at all. In fact, I find it hard to believe I was once a perfectly capable human being who made decisions all day long,' Mona piped up.

Moira nodded emphatically. 'I'm always doing it.'

'Well, that mother swan there hasn't got a mammy or older sisters looking over her shoulder telling her the baby swans need to all be in a straight line or anything has she? She can afford to be confident.'

'True enough. I'm not a fan of swans myself,' Mona supplied. 'Snappy feckers the lot of them. I was pecked by one when I was a tot.'

Moira recalled her nephew and his inability to say the letter d when he'd lost his front teeth hence he'd gone through a phase of calling the ducks something inappropriate beginning with f. She laughed at the memory of the look on her mammy's face when Noah had dropped this clanger and she relayed the story.

'I'm sure we've got it all to come,' Lisa said and Mona sat Tallulah up.

'She's finished,' she said triumphantly as she began to rub her back.

'Hello there, Tallulah,' Moira said, reaching up and stroking the baby's soft coppery head. As if aware her mammy was paying another baby attention, Kiera began to cry. 'Alright, madam, your bottle's coming.' She'd made it up before she left, knowing Kiera would be due a feed and, picking her up, she pulled a bib over her head before settling her in her arms.

Lisa stuffed the dirty nappy in a blue nappy bag and put all the baby changing paraphernalia away. 'I hope you didn't feel bad the other day at Cliona's. I noticed you left suddenly after those helpful breastfeeding comments.'

Moira shrugged.

'I hate that sort of crap,' Mona declared. 'We should support one another not try and outdo each other because we're all just trying to do our best. I don't think I'll be going along to any more of Cliona's get-togethers or whoever else puts their hand up to host a morning tea. I don't think I'd cope with hearing all about how Fenella walking at six months was a sign of superior intelligence or whatever guff your Cliona wan's likely to spout. I'd like to catch up with you two again though.'

'Me too and I won't be going again either. It wasn't my thing,' Lisa added.

Moira was totally unprepared for the dam to break and was as surprised as the others by the tears that had suddenly sprung forth.

'Moira?' Lisa inched closer and concerned, she draped an arm around her shoulder and gave it a squeeze. 'There, there. You let it all out. I shut myself in the loo the other day when Eva wouldn't stop crying and howled. I felt much better for it too. Crying at the drop of a hat is perfectly normal when you've had a baby I'm told.'

A BABY AT O'MARA'S

Kiera carried on drinking unaware of her mammy's tears. Mona fetched a packet of crumpled tissues from the pocket of her jeans and handed a wad to Moira. 'There you go. What's tipped you over the edge this morning then?'

Moira wiped her eyes, then giving Kiera a break from the bottle, she blew her nose and while she waited for the burp that would signify she was ready for more, she told them all how the unthinking remarks at the morning tea had cut deep. Then the whole christening debacle poured out on top.

'And, it's just dawned on me as to why my mammy's so upset about the morning tea not being held at O'Mara's after the service,' Moira gulped. 'And I can't believe I was so caught up in keeping Tom's mam happy I didn't think about it myself.' The something that had been bothering her had made itself crystal clear as she unburdened herself to her new friends and she sent up a silent sorry to her daddy up there in heaven.

Mona and Lisa looked at her questioningly.

'My dad died a few years back and it's because she still feels his presence at O'Mara's. He's there with us. He's part of O'Mara's and he should be part of Kiera's day.'

'You'll have to say something to Tom's mammy then,' Mona said.

'Easier said than done.' Moira didn't relish the thought of that any more than she had telling Mammy about the updated christening arrangements.

She'd fallen out with her mammy plenty of times in her life and they always made up again. She took it for granted that they'd make up but she couldn't take it for granted that she and Sylvia would if Sylvia didn't take being told the morning tea would be held at O'Mara's after all well.

215

She looked at Kiera unable to imagine how it would feel if she hurled some of the things she'd shouted at her mammy over the years to her.

She would have to ring Mammy and apologise for being insensitive, she resolved.

'As for Cliona, she behaved like a sanctimonious cow. Just because we're all new mammies doesn't mean we're going to like each other either. I mean, I wouldn't go and eat a bowl of lentils with that Meghan wan if you paid me,' Mona stated. 'And the way my mammy's behaving over Tallulah's christening you'd think it was the second coming. She's her sixth grandchild too, you'd think she'd be over it by now but no.'

Moira raised a smile.

'I overheard those two who were thick as thieves on the sofa at Cliona's whispering when she was out of the room about how one of their husbands works with Cliona's and he's a proper lad about town. Fatherhood hasn't changed him by all accounts. So don't you pay her and that daft Meghan any heed. Her life's not all that,' Lisa added. 'And the only time my mam's stopped going on about Eva's christening is when she's pointing out something I'm not doing right.'

It was lovely to know she wasn't alone in her feelings, Moira realised as Mona got to her feet.

'One good thing that came out of that coffee morning,' she said stooping to pick up Tallulah, 'is that I met you two. Now, shall we do what we came here to do and feed the ducks?'

'Yes let's go feed the fucks,' Moira lisped and Mona and Lisa laughed. The sun had come out from behind the clouds once more.

Chapter Twenty-six

It was past lunchtime when Moira returned from what had been a lovely morning with Mona, Lisa and their babies. Kiera, Tallulah and Eva had been most obliging by dropping off to sleep on their way to the coffee shop where the three mammies had all treated themselves to a hot drink and something sweet to eat.

The trio had arranged to meet a week on Saturday to catch up once more as Mona and Lisa were eager to know how Moira was getting on with college and how things had worked out with the christening arrangements.

They'd hugged goodbye and Moira had left the café feeling much brighter than she had when she'd walked out of the guesthouse earlier that morning. Problems didn't seem so insurmountable when they were shared she'd thought to herself as she'd strolled home through the Green.

The walk gave her time to think about what she would say to both Sylvia and her mammy. While she wasn't looking forward to either call she knew she'd feel much better once she'd spoken to them both and she needed to ensure Sylvia hadn't already booked the caterer she'd mentioned.

A middle-aged couple she recognised from the guesthouse were heading down the pavement toward her as she reached O'Mara's and she waited for them to catch up.

'How're you both? Are you enjoying Dublin's delights?' She smiled her greeting receiving beaming ones in return.

'Hello there, m'love, we're 'avin' a reet good olidee aren't we, Jim?' The woman who was even shorter than Moira beamed before homing in on Kiera.

'Aye reet good, lass,' Jim replied. He was dressed in the kind of causal beige chino ensemble with a jumper over his shoulders knotted at the neck that suggested his wife had had a hand in getting him dressed that morning.

It was like listening to an episode of *Emmerdale*, Moira thought, wishing Aisling were here to listen to their banter as she waited for one of them to say, I'm off t'put kettle on.

Jim opened the door and said, 'Let lass get in't door, Lucy.' He held it open for Moira.

Lucy moved aside and Moira flashed them both a grateful smile as she wheeled the pram past him. Bronagh, sitting behind the desk, had the phone pressed to her ear and spying Moira she waved out.

Lucy and Jim moved towards the front desk, obviously wanting to speak to Bronagh and Moira took advantage of them being there. 'Lucy, would you mind holding Kiera for me while I put t'pram away?' Jaysus Moira thought it was contagious, they had her at now.

'Gi her to me, lass.' Lucy held her arms out. 'There's no need for you to 'ang about looking gormless, Jim. I'll talk to Bronagh while you go put t'kettle on.'

Moira stifled a giggle as she disappeared around the corner.

Just like the Rubik's cube the pram was a lot easier to disassemble. She'd it folded and back in the cupboard in no time. Kiera was giving Lucy smiles which she was delighted by and Bronagh was looking on with an expression that could make an onion cry.

A BABY AT O'MARA'S

Moira thanked the little woman and taking her daughter back waved her tiny hand at Bronagh before heading up the stairs.

She heard Lucy call out after her, 'Ta-ra, luv.'

'Erm, ta-ra,' Moira called back.

Aisling appeared seemingly from thin air on the second-floor landing.

'Jaysus, Ash, don't be jumping out at me like a fecking Jack in the Box.' Moira came to a halt, glad she'd firm hold of her daughter.

'I didn't.' Aisling was indignant. 'I was checking Ita had made up Mr McNulty's room properly. I don't want to give him any cause for complaint.'

The air between the two sisters still held a touch of frost. Moira hesitated. She didn't find it easy to admit she'd been wrong or perhaps not wrong exactly but definitely hasty in agreeing to everything Sylvia had suggested for the christening. She licked her lips as she tried to formulate what it was she wanted to say but in the end blurted, 'I had time to think about, you know, what I mentioned earlier, walking back from meeting the girls.'

Aisling raised an eyebrow. 'Oh yes?' She tapped a foot, impatient to crack on with the long list of jobs she'd written on her to-do list but wanting to hear what Moira had to say too.

'Yes, and I think the morning tea should be held here at O'Mara's after all.'

Aisling was nodding in the dim light of the floor where she was standing. 'Good. What changed your mind then?'

'Daddy did,' Moira said.

'Oh.' Aisling didn't need to ask her what she meant because she already knew. A lump formed in her throat. 'Daddy would like that very much and I'm sure it will go a long way to appeasing Mammy.'

'I hope so.'

'Quinn was hoping to cater the morning tea for you and Tom you know.'

'I didn't know that.'

'Well, you didn't give him a chance to mention it did you? And I didn't see the point in saying anything earlier.'

'It's very kind of him.'

'Not at all. You, Tom and Kiera are family, of course he wants to do the food.'

The frosty air evaporated as quickly as it had descended and Aisling came over to tickle her niece's cheek before wishing Moira luck with Mammy and heading down the stairs.

The apartment was as quiet as it had been when she'd left earlier and she put the radio on while she fed and changed Kiera, all the while singing along softly to what was being played. Kiera gazed up at her adoringly and Moira's heart melted as it did each time her daughter locked eyes with her. It was a bonus that she liked her mammy's singing too.

'Right then, Miss Kiera, time for you to have a stretch under the gym,' Moira said, picking Kiera up and placing her on the mat under the arch with all of its whizz-bang attachments. 'I've a couple of phone calls to make. Wish me luck.'

Kiera broke wind and Moira laughed.

A BABY AT O'MARA'S

She made herself a cup of tea and then sat at the table. She stared at the telephone in her hand for a moment and then rang her mammy.

Donal answered and, good man that he was, didn't sound at all put out even though she knew he'd have copped it in the ear the night before after her conversation with Mammy.

'She's quilting with her quilting group, Moira, but I'm sure she'd love to hear from you. Why don't you give her a ring on her mobile?'

'I will do, thanks, Donal.'

'Oh, and, Moira, how are you placed to go for a drive on Saturday afternoon?'

'That would be grand, thanks a million, Donal.' Moira straightened in the seat. She'd have her licence in no time. Kiera gurgled and she waved over at her before ringing her mammy's mobile number.

'Hello there, can you hear me? You've reached Maureen O'Mara's mobile phone.' She'd nearly had an accident when she'd realised it was her phone ringing in the church hall where she was sat at a table opposite Rosemary working on her memory quilt.

'Mammy, it's me, Moira.' She decided as this was a conciliatory phone call she'd not go on about her telephone manner.

'Moira? Would that be my youngest daughter Moira who hung up on her mammy last night? Is that to whom I'm speaking?'

Moira gritted her teeth. She'd known Mammy wouldn't make it easy for her. 'Yes, Mammy, it would be that Moira.'

'And what can I do for you then?'

Best she come right out with it, Moira decided. 'I'm ringing to say, erm what is it...' The word wouldn't come.

'Moira, I'm quilting. I've not got all day.'

Moira swallowed hard. 'I'm sorry about last night, Mammy.'

Maureen started coughing and Moira heard Rosemary say she'd fetch her a glass of water.

'Mammy?'

'Did you say you were sorry?'

'I did and I am.' Moira blinked. It hadn't been that hard after all.

Maureen over in Howth was blinking in disbelief too. She'd been wrong she thought. Motherhood had changed Moira after all.

'I didn't think things through and I was worried about offending Sylvia by saying no to her ideas.' She didn't like to add, especially given Sylvia and her husband were paying for it all.

There was a snort. 'I see but you don't think twice about offending your mammy? Your own flesh and blood.'

'Mammy, you're not being very gracious.' Moira was all about being gracious of late. It had been a weak point but one she'd been working on.

Maureen's bristles flattened down. Moira had apologised after all. Rome wasn't built in a day and all that.

'It feels as though Daddy will be with us if we have the afters here at O'Mara's.'

Maureen's blinking became more rapid and Rosemary wondered if she'd something in her eye. Moira had hit a home run straight to her heart with that remark.

A BABY AT O'MARA'S

'So how about a compromise, Mammy?' Moira held her breath; compromise and Mammy did not go together.

'Yees,' Maureen dragged the word out uncertainly.

'How about the church service is held over there in Blanchardstown but the morning tea is held back here at O'Mara's. Aisling's just told me Quinn was wanting to cater it, which is very kind of him. I figure if people want to be part of Kiera's day they won't mind travelling between venues. Oh, and I could have a word with Father Fitzpatrick about coming here for a bite to eat after he's finished his Sunday service. You know how partial he is to a sausage roll or two.'

'Or three,' Maureen added. He erred toward being greedy when it came to the party plates of food at church suppers. She studied the work in progress draped over her lap. She knew she'd two options. She could accept Moira's suggested compromise graciously or she could be difficult.

Her eyes settled on the square she'd been in the process of stitching onto the cot quilt when her mobile had rung. It was a piece of material from Moira's own christening gown.

She thought back on Moira's christening at St Theresa's. It had been a lovely day and she'd looked a picture but what a headache she'd had leading up to it thanks to her mam. Their relationship had been strained anyway after Maureen had left home and run off to Dublin. She'd patched it up to the point of civility when the children had come along but there were times like when she'd been arranging Moira's christening she was almost sorry she'd bothered.

Her mam had harped on and on about it being a nuisance having to travel from Ballyclegg for the christening until finally Brian had put his foot down. He'd said she should tell her mammy to either come or not come. It was up to her, and then she should let it go because Moira was their daughter, and therefore it wasn't about her mam.

Maureen didn't want to be like her mam spoiling things for her daughter and this was why she opened her mouth and said graciously, 'That sounds a grand plan indeed, Moira.'

Moira did the blinking again and then, remembering they were being gracious, told her mammy she was delighted she thought so.

She'd another call to make now she'd come this far, and so saying goodbye to Mammy, she rang Sylvia. The phone was answered after four rings.

'Hello, Sylvia, it's Moira.'

'Moira, hello, darling, how are you? How's Kiera and my Tom?'

'Grand, all grand, thanks. Have you time for a quick word?'

'I do. Oh, before I forget I've had the christening cards printed.'

'Yes, about that—'

Chapter Twenty-seven

Moira raised her foot out of the suds and inspected her toes. The nail varnish she'd gotten Aisling to apply a few days before she'd gone into labour had all but chipped off. Her feet were not what you'd call summer ready.

She reached forward to turn the hot tap on for a top-up. Soaking in the bath and chatting to Andrea was taking her newly found multitasking skills to a whole other level. It could have been worse, she thought glancing over at the toilet. She pressed the phone closer to her ear to hear Andrea over the running water.

'And what did Tom's mammy say when you told her that she'd have to change all the invitations because the morning tea was going to be served at O'Mara's?' she asked.

'To be fair she was very good about it all. I was honest with her and told her that now I'd had a chance to think it all through I'd realised it would mean a lot to Mammy and all of us to have the gathering here. I told her if Daddy couldn't be with us in the flesh then at least we'd feel he was there watching over us in spirit. She said she could understand that and she was sorry if she'd been too gung-ho with all the arrangements. I think Tom might have already had a quiet word with her.'

'Well, it was very good of her given she'd already begun making the arrangements. You don't want to be falling out with her this early in the piece.'

Moira agreed with her.

'Why does your voice sound strange?'

'Because the clay mask I put on is drying and it's getting hard to move my mouth. I'm making the most of Tom having a night off and taking charge. I might even shave my legs. I feel a little selfish though, Tom's shattered too and could probably do with a hot bath himself.'

'So long as he doesn't come and join you while I'm on the phone thanks very much.'

Moira laughed. 'Chance would be a fine thing. My legs are like the Black Forest at the moment. Did I tell you what Mona said she overheard two of the mammy's talking about at that awful morning tea I went to?'

Andrea sighed. 'Yes you did and I hope you haven't forgotten who is senior godmother of your child now you've got all these new mammy friends to be getting about with.'

She had been going on about them, Moira supposed and her and Andrea's lives were at very different stages but they'd shared a lot of good times and she was still her best friend. 'Sorry. Baby brain.'

'Fair play.'

'Would you help me choose a dress to wear to the christening? I don't think my red floaty one that Tom loves and Mammy goes mad over will go down well with the parishioners of St Mary's.'

Andrea snorted, 'The old Moira would have had no qualms about flashing her knickers in church.'

It was true enough, Moira mused. 'But, I've Kiera to think of now. I don't want her looking back on her christening photos and wondering why her mammy is exposing herself in a

A BABY AT O'MARA'S

holy place. Besides, the big knickers I've been wearing since she was born would give you nightmares.'

'I bet they're comfy so.' Andrea sounded wistful. She was looking forward to the day she settled down and could discard all her lacy thongs in favour of a cotton five-pack.

'They are but don't tell my mammy that or I'll be inundated with sensible knickers come Christmas.'

Andrea laughed. 'When were you thinking of going shopping then?'

'Saturday morning if you're free. I've a driving lesson with Donal, good man that he is, in the afternoon.'

'Good on you. I am free, and I'd like that. I'll choose something to wear too because I want to look like I'm taking my new role as godmother seriously but drop-dead gorgeous at the same time.'

They chatted over appropriate dresses for christenings and the finer points of gear changing and how the indicator lever was similar to the windscreen wiper one and who was the eejit who designed that? Then Moira remembered what else she had to tell her friend.

'I can't believe I nearly forgot to tell you.'

'Tell me what?'

'Tom has a cousin.'

'Bully for him. I've hundreds of the feckers, one lurking in every village in Ireland.'

'No not a cousin from the boondocks of Ballywherever. A good-looking single cousin who is coming up from Limerick for the christening because Tom's asked him to be godfather alongside Quinn. He and Tom get on very well. He showed me a photo of the pair of them acting the maggot when they were younger the other night.'

'There's good looking and then there's *good* looking. What league are we talking? Tom good looking or yer man I pointed out to you busking on Grafton Street who I said was cute?'

'We're talking Tom Cruise good looking. I've seen a photo. I can confirm he's gorgeous.'

'And he's single?'

'He is.'

'Why?' Andrea was instantly suspicious. 'Does he have the halitosis?'

'No.' Moira had no idea whether he did or he didn't. 'Tom said he had a long-term girlfriend but they split up halfway through last year. I'm sure Tom said it was him that broke it off so it wasn't because of his halitosis or anything.'

'But, you said he doesn't have halitosis.'

'He doesn't and would you shut up and let me finish.'

'Alright, but if he does have the smelly breath I'm holding you responsible.'

Moira ignored her. 'He's been happily single but lately, he's been making noises about wanting to meet someone and settle down. I think it's because Tom has.'

'Really? He wants to settle down? He sounds too good to be true. You'll be telling me he likes long walks on the beach next.'

'Andrea, do you remember when we got collared at the Boots for shoplifting and yer man Connor Reid saw us get hauled off by security?'

A BABY AT O'MARA'S

'I will never live that down and we weren't shoplifting we just forgot to pay is all. How could I forget it? Connor still gives me pitying looks when I see him around the office.'

'I promised you I'd make things right and this is me making things right.'

Andrea decided not to look a gift horse in the mouth. 'Right, well I'm going to need a fact file. Name, age, employment, interests that sort of thing so as I can hold a sparkling conversation with him about whatever it is he's into so long as it's not the hurling. I can't stand the hurling all that running around on a muddy field with a wooden stick.' She paused to draw breath. 'Or the uilleann pipes. They'd make me want to throw myself into the Liffey they would.'

'Me too and I've already gathered all the necessary personal information and there's no hurling or uilleann pipes. His name's Declan Daly, he's twenty-nine years old and solidly built on account of his running a building company.'

'Eyes?'

'Blue.'

'Hair?'

'Brown nearly black and his interests are playing squash and running marathons.'

'For feck's sake why couldn't he have been into a sedentary pursuit like bird watching? You know what this means, don't you?'

'What?'

'I'm going to have to get myself some proper sports shoes tomorrow lunchtime. I'd my sights set on a new pair of boots. Feck!'

Moira nearly dropped the phone. 'Andrea don't screech like that I nearly lost the phone in the bath.

'You'd screech too if you'd only three weeks to learn the rules of squash and start training for the Dublin marathon.'

'You hate running though. You won't even run for the bus.'

'Moira, sometimes sacrifices have to be made for the greater good.'

'God loves a trier, Andrea.' Moira giggled then announced she had to go because Tom would be putting Kiera to bed and she wanted to get the face pack off and prune the Black Forest just in case he decided to join her for an ahem, soak.

'Too much information,' Andrea said ringing off.

Moira sank down under the bubbles feeling blissfully happy with her lot.

Chapter Twenty-eight

Nina dangled the coloured rings she'd bought for Kiera over her and smiled as she waved her plump arms about, tracking them with a happy smile. She was such a beautiful baby, she thought. Moira was a lucky woman.

This was her first Wednesday looking after Kiera and she was proving an easy baby. She'd told Moira there was no need to telephone and check how she was getting on because if there were any problems she would ring her. Moira had paid no attention though and had been ringing every hour on the hour. Nina didn't mind. She was the same when Ana was a baby.

She glanced at her watch. Moira had left step by step instructions of Kiera's routine pinned to the fridge and according to that, she was due her bottle in fifteen minutes. Then it would be time for a story and after that, she should sleep for three hours or so.

Nina would have her lunch then and after that, she didn't know. The idea of sitting around doing nothing until her charge woke went against her nature and she glanced around the apartment. It could do with a vacuum and perhaps a dust. She knew the dishwasher needed emptying, she could do that too.

Her pen and notepad were in her bag, she'd write to Elena too and tell her about her new Wednesday job. The time would pass quickly enough.

She jumped as her mobile rang and, setting the rings down, she scrambled to retrieve it from her bag. It hardly ever rang. She hoped it wasn't Pedro wanting to know if she could fill in for one of the other waitresses. He was used to her being readily available but today she was otherwise occupied.

'Ola, this is Nina.'

'Nina.' A familiar voice said her name and Nina felt a stab of fear over what this uncharacteristic telephone call might mean.

'Mama, is everything alright? Papa, Ana?'

'Nina, calm yourself. It is Ana—'

'What is it, what's happened?'

'She's alright now, but she's broken her arm.'

Nina's heart threatened to jump right out of her shirt. 'But how? And you say she's alright?'

'Si, she will be fine. She fell off the swings in the playground, showing off how she could jump off while she was still swinging. Your papa, he took her to hospital and they put it in a cast. The break is straightforward but she'll have to wear a cast for six weeks.'

'Oh, Mama.'

'Nina, listen to your mother, she is fine. She will mend. Your papa said I should wait until tonight when you were home to telephone you but I said no, she is her mama, she should know.'

'Gracias, Mama.' A tear trickled down Nina's cheek, she should be there. 'Can I speak to her?'

'Ana, your mama wants to talk to you.'

It was all Nina could do not to sob as a little voice said, 'Ola, Mama.'

A BABY AT O'MARA'S

'Ana, tell me you're alright?'

She managed a weak smile as her daughter cheerily lisped her way through the events of the afternoon with the highlight being the lollipop she was given by the nurse while she waited for the cast to set.

'Mama, when will you come home? You need to put your name on my cast. Yayo and Abue have and the nice lollipop nurse. Now I need you to sign your name on my cast.'

Nina's heart broke that her parents had done this but she couldn't. I should be there, she said to herself balling her hand into a fist and thumping her thigh in frustration.

'Mama?'

She heard her mother asking for the telephone and she came back on saving Nina from replying to a question she didn't know how to answer. 'This call is very expensive, Nina.'

'I understand. Thank you, Mama, for ringing to tell me.' A sob caught in her throat, and her mother's voice was soft when she replied.

'We love her too, Nina. She's safe with us. I must say adios.'

'I know that Mama but she's my daughter,' Nina said but the line had gone dead.

She allowed herself to cry properly then. She should be there. Her daughter needed her and instead, she was here looking after someone else's child.

Chapter Twenty-nine

Moira had been back at college for three whole days and to her amazement, she was loving it. She'd even managed to stay awake throughout the day but then again she mused it was different when you were doing something you loved. Art was her passion. If she'd been doing the algebra or something like that she'd have been snoring before the morning break.

That wasn't to say she didn't miss Kiera but it helped to know she was being looked after by people who loved her. She'd rung Mammy at regular intervals on Monday. Mammy had raised her voice to her after the fourth call and said she was beginning to think the mobile phone was a menace and could she not feed the ducks in peace with her granddaughter?

The best thing of all about college was the anticipation of going home to hold Kiera at the end of the day. The bubbling joy of breathing in her milky sweet, baby smell when she arrived home would threaten to overflow.

She'd fully intended to leave Nina in peace today, but her fingers had taken on a life of their own, hitting speed dial for home whenever she got the chance. The Spanish girl had promised to phone Moira if she had any problems whatsoever and had told her she'd plenty of experience looking after babies, but despite her reassurances, Moira had been unable to help herself.

A BABY AT O'MARA'S

Bronagh had given up collaring her for a chat at the end of the day when she breezed in through the door, calling out hello as she took to the stairs as though training for the steeplechase.

Today, as she climbed them, her neck ached from being bent over her current work in progress and she'd be glad to offload her art satchel. She was already sliding it from her shoulder as she reached the apartment, and opening the door, she dumped it just inside the entrance. 'Hello,' she called announcing her arrival home.

'Ola, Moira,' was called back.

Moira frowned walking through to the living room, Nina's voice sounded odd and she found her sitting cross-legged on the floor by the baby gym. Her wallet was open in front of her as she stared at a picture inside it.

Her boyfriend perhaps, Moira mused although she'd never mentioned one, but then Nina kept herself to herself.

Nina snapped the wallet shut and shoved it in her pocket as she got to her feet brushing non-existent lint from her jeans. 'I hope you had a good day at college, Moira. Kiera has been a dream bebé. I put her down for a sleep about thirty minutes ago. Like you said to do on there.' She gestured to the fridge.

She definitely sounded odd, Moira thought, taking note of Nina's face; it was blotchy red against the olive hue. 'Are you alright?' Perhaps she'd broken up with her fella.

Nina's eyes welled at the compassion on Moira's face.

'Nina, what is it?' Moira was getting worried now.

She shook her dark hair and sniffed wishing she had a tissue to hand. 'I must go. Adios.' She moved to pick up the leather backpack she carried with her everywhere.

'No, wait. Let me make you a cup of tea.'

These Irish thought a cup of tea fixed everything Nina thought but she hesitated. It was hard carrying the weight of missing Ana around on her own.

Moira, sensing her hesitancy told her to go and sit down while she set about making a brew. She glanced over her shoulder at Nina whose hands were clasped as she stared down at them from where she sat on the sofa.

'I'll just check on Kiera while the tea steeps,' she said once she'd poured the water onto the teabags.

Nina raised a smile.

Moira pushed open the door to the bedroom the three of them shared and saw in the semi-darkened room the mound of her daughter in the cot. She tiptoed over and rested her hand on her warm tummy. Kiera stirred and flung her arms over her head having freed them from the sheet she was wrapped in. Moira held her breath but she didn't wake and, satisfied all was as it should be, she crept from the room closing the door behind her.

'Here we are,' she said to Nina a minute later. 'I put a sugar in yours because Mammy always says a teaspoon of sugar in a strong cup of tea sorts anyone out.'

'Gracias.'

Moira sat down next to her and kicked her shoes off before folding her legs under herself. She picked up her steaming mug and blew on it, taking a tentative sip while she waited to see if Nina would confide as to what had her feeling sad.

Nina's hand shook as she reached for her tea. She mimicked Moira's actions and took a sip of the hot, sweet liquid before putting it down on the coaster and saying, 'I have a bebé too.'

A BABY AT O'MARA'S

Moira nearly spilt her tea. This was news to her. Not once in the time Nina had worked here at the guesthouse had she mentioned anyone back home other than her mother and father.

Nina shrugged. 'I never told you because I feel bad for leaving her in Spain.'

'But you must have your reasons.' Moira tried to keep the surprise off her face. She couldn't fathom leaving Kiera to go to another country but she didn't want to judge Nina either before she heard what she had to say.

'She's four. I hadn't even finished school when I had her. I had such big plans, you know.'

Moira nodded. She did know. She'd been derailed when she found out she was pregnant but she'd never had any doubt she wanted her baby. She knew, even though there'd been times she'd resented her mammy and Sylvia's input, she was fortunate to have their support. There was no way she'd be able to finish her studies without them.

She'd assumed Nina was around her own age but from what she'd just told her she had to be around twenty-one. This surprised her, not because she looked older than this but rather she'd always seemed older. She'd a wise aura about her.

'I never once regretted Ana though.'

'Ana, that's a pretty name.'

Nina smiled. 'Si. She's my world but you know I have no qualifications and nothing to give her when she's older other than what my parents will give me.'

'The restaurant.' Moira filled in for her.

'Si, Abello's. Ana's father, he doesn't even know she exists.' She told Moira the story of the Italian backpacker who'd come to stay and who'd unknowingly left so much behind in Toledo. 'I don't know anything about him other than he is from Rome.' Nina shrugged again. 'I don't know how I will tell her this when the time comes. It was a summer of madness. But now you understand, si? Why I must do what I can to help my parents with the restaurant. It was their livelihood and now it's mine and Ana's too.' Nina closed her eyes for a moment remembering that long ago afternoon when she'd dragged her feet reluctantly home.

Toledo 1996

IF BRANDO HAD CARRIED on to Granada as he'd planned then she'd never have given herself to him.

She blamed those romance novels of Elena's mother. It was thanks to those silly paperbacks that she'd had her head in the clouds waiting for her tall, dark, handsome stranger to arrive in town and sweep her off her feet. That was why when he'd come back, she'd allowed herself to be swept up in her own torrid romance.

Brando had gone as far as the bus station at the bottom of the hill before making his way back up it to Abello's.

His reason for staying another two nights, he told Nina, was so he could spend a little more time with the beautiful daughter of the restaurant owners who served the best cocida madrileño in all of Spain.

Si, she thought to herself, watching her mama. If he'd left when he was supposed to then she wouldn't be standing here now.

A BABY AT O'MARA'S

She breathed in the sulphurous odour of the onions her mother was chopping and the smell turned her stomach and made her eyes burn.

The knife her mother kept razor sharp glinted as it rocked up and down making light work of the pile of peeled raw onions. Nina knew her mother's eyes would have teared up which was why she hadn't registered her standing in the shadows of the doorway.

It was an anomaly that she hadn't built up an immunity to onions after all these years, Nina thought, although she was grateful at this moment in time she hadn't. Even if it was only a momentary reprieve from the inevitable.

'Go get changed, Nina,' she bossed not pausing in her slicing.

Nina blinked. She hadn't thought she'd seen her but she should know by now her mother had eyes in the back of her head. She didn't move, opening her mouth to say what she had to say but the words wouldn't come.

Her mother put down the knife and turned to look at her. Her face was pink with the heat from the kitchen and there were tear tracks down both cheeks. She'd sweaty rounds under her arms forming two perfect arcs and a white apron that had seen better days wrapped around her soft middle. Her father had yet to come downstairs.

'What is it? Are you sick, you look a little peaky? Come here I will feel your forehead.'

Nina shook her head although she felt sick. The words fell out of her mouth. 'I'm not sick, Mama, I'm pregnant.' Nina was glad her mother had put down the knife because had she been holding it in her hand she surely would have dropped it and she might have injured herself. The loose bun she pulled her hair back into when she was working in the kitchen threatened to come undone as she shook her head. 'No, it is not possible. You're not funny, Nina.'

'Mama, I'm not being funny.' Nina began to cry then and through her tears saw her mother's face pale as the reality of what she'd just been told sank in.

She shrieked for her husband then and Nina wished with all her heart that she could click her fingers and be anywhere but where she was at that moment in time.

Her father's steps thundered down the stairs and he burst into the kitchen, panic etched on his face. 'What is it? What's happened?' His dark eyes flew from his wife to his daughter.

Her mother burst into noisy tears and she pointed at Nina. 'You tell him.'

'Tell me what,' he demanded.

'Oh, Papa I'm sorry...'

'I THINK TELLING MY mother and my father I was pregnant was the hardest thing I've ever had to do in my life,' Nina told Moira. 'The second hardest was telling them that I didn't know how to contact Brando.'

Moira was sitting with her head tilted to one side imagining how the teenage Nina must have felt.

'But once the shock wore off they came round. They ignored the shaking heads and wagging tongues and eventually people got sick of whispering and pointing behind our backs.

A BABY AT O'MARA'S

Then, when Ana was born, they fell in love with her just like I did. She is lucky to have so much love.'

'So, why so sad today, Nina? Is it homesickness?' Moira asked.

She nodded and told her about the phone call and how her heart was breaking because she wanted more than anything to be home with her little girl.

'Nina, you must go home. Aisling will understand.'

Nina shook her head. 'No, we are so close if I go home now the extension will still be out of reach and this here,' she threw her hands up, 'will have been for nothing.'

Moira thought for a moment and then Lisa's words came back to her. 'Someone told me the other day that the best advice they've been given as a mammy is to trust your own instinct when it comes to your baby or child.' It was something Moira knew she needed to begin doing herself. 'What does your instinct tell you should do?'

'Instinct?' she shook her head, 'I do not know this word.'

Moira patted her stomach. 'Your gut.'

'Ah.' Nina was quiet for a moment. 'It says Ana needs me and I should go home.'

'Then that's what you have to do.'

Nina looked at Moira; she made it sound so simple but perhaps it could be as simple as that. Maybe Ana having broken her arm was God's way of telling her she should go home.

Chapter Thirty

Three weeks later, the day of the Christening

Moira picked up the envelope postmarked Spain from the table where Aisling had left it along with the pile of other cards that had arrived from those that weren't able to attend the christening today.

'We'll have to leave in a minute,' Tom said, tucking his shirt into his suit pants as he appeared in the living room. 'What's my hair like? Aisling's still in the bathroom so I couldn't wet it and smooth it down.'

'She's a bathroom hog that one, anyone would think it was her big day,' Moira said, temporarily forgetting the envelope she had in her hand as she soaked in the rare sight of Tom in a suit. 'And your hair looks like you just shook it dry at the beach but that's the way I like it.' She twirled in her new dress. 'What do you think?'

Tom gave a long low whistle. 'You scrub up well, Ms O'Mara.'

Moira smoothed the ruched middle of her mauve wrap dress which covered her knees and did wonders for her post-baby tummy. It wasn't designer and it hadn't been expensive but still, she felt a million dollars in it. She hoped Mammy wouldn't make a thing out of them both being converts to the wrap dress and the big knickers.

A BABY AT O'MARA'S

It was Kiera who was the star of the show today though she thought, glancing over to where she was propped up by cushions on the sofa dressed in her christening finery. The Pooh Bear bib she'd had on was at odds with her dress but Moira was taking no risks. She watched her daughter suck on her dimpled fist.

She was fed, changed, and Moira had high hopes of her lasting the service and holding it together long enough for the photos afterwards.

The dress Sylvia had picked out did look beautiful and the bonnet had grown on her Moira decided. She'd the little silver expandable bracelet on her wrist too. She and Tom had picked it out at the jewellers and had it engraved, determined to splurge on a keepsake for their daughter's day.

'Doesn't she look a picture?'

Tom beamed proudly. 'I'm a lucky man to have two such beautiful girls in my life that's for sure.'

'I got a couple of photos before I put the bib on her but we'd best leave it on now until we get to St Mary's just in case.'

Tom nodded and gestured to the envelope again.

Moira had forgotten she had it in her hand. 'I think it's from Nina,' she said opening it and pulling out the card upon which a Spanish verse was surrounded by a silver frame. She opened it and scanned the text inside eager for news.

'It is from Nina,' she confirmed as she began to read the small, neat script.

'That was good of her to remember,' Tom said.

Moira nodded. 'She wishes us well for our day and says she's happy to be home.' Surprise registered on her face.

'What?' Tom asked.

Moira opened and shut her eyes rapidly to ensure she'd read the message correctly before closing the card and looking at Tom. 'She's written that a few days after she arrived home an anonymous cheque postmarked Ireland arrived. It was enough to cover the shortfall for the restaurant extension, work's beginning on it next week.'

'That's brilliant but who'd have sent that?' Tom frowned, puzzled.

'She said she thinks it came from an Irish Angel.' Moira thought for a moment. Mammy had been upset for Nina when she'd relayed what their night receptionist had told her about her reasons for working two jobs here in Ireland. She cast her mind back remembering how she'd shook her head and said it wasn't right. 'I have a feeling it was a Mo-pant wearing angel who lives in a house with a—'

'Sea view,' Tom finished for her. 'What a kind thing to do.'

Moira murmured her agreement. A pain in the arse her mammy might well be but she was kind from the top of her head to the tip of those eyesore boat shoes she was fond of wearing. She stood the card up on the table as Tom searched around for his car keys and stalked to the bathroom.

'Oi, Aisling, get yer arse out of there now. I need a wee.'

***

MOIRA WAS PLEASED NO other babies were being christened that morning at St Mary's, an old stone church with clumps of daffodils decorating either side of the path leading to the entrance. It meant Kiera wouldn't have to share the limelight. She was also pleased that the sun was shining for the photographs that would be taken on the church steps after the service.

She cast about for her daughter having lost track of which relative was asking to have a 'go' of the baby next and how many times she'd heard, 'doesn't she look a wee angel,' since they'd arrived at the church.

Sylvia, who looked glamorous but not over the top in a mint-coloured dress was having a chat with Mammy who'd not let go of Patrick since he'd arrived from Los Angeles. He had to dodge the peacock feather protruding from the side of Mammy's hat, which was anything but understated, whenever she bobbed her head in agreement with whatever Sylvia was talking about. Donal was laughing at something Jim, Tom's father was saying.

Moira reached out and caught Aisling's sleeve bringing her to a standstill. 'Would you make sure she's behaving herself?' She gestured her head towards Mammy. Aisling obliged, tottering off in her new Louboutin's. Quinn was talking to Andrea who kept looking over his shoulder in the hope of spying a good-looking, fit fella. So far it was slim pickings in the church, she thought, scowling at Moira's leery uncle who was waggling his eyebrows suggestively at her.

Roisin was busy trying to keep Noah away from their great aunt Rosemary. The woman was a notorious sloppy kisser and cheek grabber. She managed to grab a minute with Noah wanting to make a fuss of him. He had excitedly told her about Mr Nibbles' new friend, Steve who had come to live with him.

Her uncle Colin appeared to be channelling his inner Elton John with the bright yellow framed glasses he'd chosen to wear, Moira thought. She noticed most of the women in the congregation were struggling to tear their gazes from Ricardo, looking like Ricky Martin in a suit. Emer, for one, kept invading his personal space.

It was a very special trip for Uncle Colin as it was the first time he'd brought his partner with him to the country of his birth.

Bronagh however only had eyes for Leonard and she looked lovely in her two-piece pink outfit with fascinator; she'd had her roots done for the occasion too.

Moira's eyes narrowed as she homed in on Uncle Frankie and Uncle Brendan although to be fair they appeared to be the best of pals laughing and joking together. How long that would last was anyone's bet, Moira thought, eyeing her mam's brothers. Speaking of bets, Uncle Colm had opened a book on whether or not the baby would cry at the altar. She shot him a dirty look but he didn't notice, too busy taking a wad of notes off Great Aunt Noreen. As for Uncle Tom, he was hunched over in his pew having a surreptitious pick of his nose.

Father Simon was clearing his throat and Kiera was passed from one to the other until she arrived back in her mammy's arms. They all sat down in the pews lining either side of the aisle, the O'Mara family, Kiera's godparents and the Dalys in the front row. One person was missing though.

'Where is he, Tom?' Andrea asked leaning over Moira and Kiera.

'Who?'

'Your cousin, Declan of course.'

They both did a sweep of the pews to where Quinn was looking very po-faced at the gravitas of the role he was about to

A BABY AT O'MARA'S

undertake as were Tom's brothers but of their fellow godfather, there was no sign.

'Typical Declan, he's always cutting it fine. Don't worry he'll be here.'

The church door opened and heads swivelled to see who the late-comer was.

It was like in the films where they do the slow-motion thing, Andrea thought, as she zeroed in on the handsome fella with dark hair and blue eyes breezing up the aisle waving out to family members. There might as well have been nobody else in the church at that moment because all Andrea could see was him as she flicked her hair back and smiled her most seductive smile. He shook Tom's hand heartily and apologised for running late as he sat down alongside Quinn and introduced himself.

'I'm Andrea, I'm training for the Dublin marathon,' she said leaning over Moira once more. Declan's eyes flickered with interest but Father Simon was clearing his throat once more and looked pointedly at those whispering in the front row.

Maureen leaned forward and mimed, zip it, at Andrea who did so, having no wish to get offside with Mrs O'Mara.

A hush descended broken only by Noah's, 'Mammy I need the toilet. It's a number two.'

Jaysus wept, Moira thought.

THE GUESTS' LOUNGE of O'Mara's off to the side of the reception area where young James was manning the phones in between enjoying the plate of savouries Maureen had whisked out to him, was heaving. Any curious guest who'd poked their head around their door to see what was going on was welcomed in to join them and told there was plenty of food. Quinn had done them proud.

The buzz of conversation and laughter filled the room and the phrase, 'Sure wasn't she a good baby,' was bandied about. The only surly faces belonged to those who'd bet there'd be tears at the font.

The service had gone very well Moira thought, hoping the incident where Andrea and Bronagh had jostled one another in a bid to stand next to Moira and Kiera at the font hadn't been caught on the video Patrick had taken. Aisling had stepped in between them and kept them in their place.

Moira began to make her way over to the corner of the room where Kiera, who'd gone to sleep on the way back from the service, had been placed. She chatted to guests, some of whom she knew, some of whom she'd only just been introduced to and caught Tom's wink, shooting a full wattage smile back at him. Out of the corner of her eye, she spied Andrea demonstrating her squash swing and she winced as her friend narrowly missed sending the heaped plateful of savouries Father Fitzpatrick was about to tuck into flying.

Aisling she saw, was tending to Great Aunt Noreen who'd been poked in the eye by the peacock feather protruding from Mammy's hat.

'Oi, Rosi,' she said interrupting her sister who was having a deep and meaningful with Shay. 'Have you been introduced to this cousin Sheridan and Great Aunt Dolly of ours yet?' She wanted to be certain Mammy hadn't made them up.

A BABY AT O'MARA'S

Roisin's eyes had a daft love-struck sheen to them as she shook her head and Moira left them to it, her suspicions mounting. Noah was running around with Donal's daughter Louise's children and their aunt Anna was trying to quieten them down. She wondered how long it would be before they were all going for rides in the dumbwaiter.

Kiera she saw, at last reaching her daughter, was still sound asleep. There was a tap on her shoulder and she turned around to see the vision in blue-green peering out from under her hat that was her mammy.

'I've something for you.' She was holding a parcel out to her.

The occasional table by the window and the floor around it was stacked with gifts for Kiera and Moira wondered why she hadn't put it there to be opened later.

'I want to see your face when you open it.'

Moira was about to do just that when she remembered what she'd asked Roisin. 'Mammy, point out my second cousin Sheridan and Great Aunt Dolly would you? I'd like to meet them.'

Maureen, hat angled just so, looked more shifty than mysterious as she inclined her head toward the door and said, 'You just missed them, they've had to go home as Aunt Dolly's got to see to the sheep and Sheridan drove them here. They've a long drive home ahead of them, so.'

'You made all of that up, Mammy.'

'I did not. Your Great Aunt Dolly's President of the Claredonkelly Sheep Association so she is, she took over from your Great Uncle Oisin.' She shook the present. 'Open it.'

Moira didn't believe a word of it but curiosity got the better of her and she did as she was told, tearing into the paper and unfolding the cot-sized quilt inside. She stared hard at it. The joins were clumsy but it was the squares of fabric comprising it that were holding her attention.

'Mammy, is that blanky?' she asked.

Maureen nodded. 'It is and that square there is from your christening gown, and that's from your first uniform in the senior school. It's a memory quilt so it is.'

Moira held the quilt to her face and breathed in the scent of her childhood. 'I love it, Mammy, thank you.'

Maureen puffed up with pleasure seeing her daughter's face alight with wonder. 'I wanted you to have it today. Although, I'll have to take it back when the judging begins on the Memories section of the Annual Quilters Association competition.'

'Fair play, Mammy.'

'She looks just like you when you were that age, you know,' she said, smiling down at her sleeping granddaughter.

'Does she?'

'She does. I remember looking at you on your christening day wondering what you'd be like when you grew up and look at you here now, all grown up with a baby of your own. The years go by very fast, so they do. Make the most of them, Moira. Time's precious.' Maureen's eyes misted. 'I'm proud of you and your daddy would have been too.'

'Do you think so?'

'I know so. You're doing a grand job so you are.'

Mammy was right, Moira decided. Time did go fast and she didn't want to waste any more of it worrying as to whether she was getting this mammy business right. She was doing her best and that was what mattered.

Maureen patted her arm and spying her brother Frank pouring the whiskey into his tea she made a beeline over there to sort him out.

Kiera picked that moment to open her eyes and she fixed them on her mammy.

'I'm doing a good job aren't I, Kiera?' Moira said, crouching down in front of her.

The gummy smile she was rewarded with was the only answer needed.

The End.

A BABY AT O'MARA'S

The Housewarming, Book 11, The Guesthouse on the Green is available in paperback and kindle on 28 November, 2021. www.michellevernalbooks.com

Printed in Great Britain
by Amazon